MW01234847

A WEEK AWAY

A DOM REILLY MYSTERY

MARSHALL THORNTON

Published by Kenmore Books

Edited by Joan Martinelli

Cover design by Marshall Thornton

Images by 123rf stock

ISBN:978-1-965306-03-1

First Edition

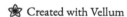 Created with Vellum

ACKNOWLEDGMENTS

A big thank you to: Joan Martinelli, John Adams, Pekka Mackoin, Tina Greene Bevington, and Lorri Wallet.

PROLOGUE

Fall 1978

"What are we going to do?" the girl asked. She was nearly seventeen, pretty, with long black hair and dark eyes. She wore a fuzzy lavender jacket, a pair of high-waisted jeans, and platform saddle shoes.

The man with her was twenty-three, twenty-four at the most, with washed-out blue eyes and floppy brown hair. He wore a plaid cloth jacket and bell-bottom jeans. "I wish you'd told me how old you were. It wasn't nice to lie to me."

"I wanted you to like me."

They were wandering around Belle Isle Conservatory. A seventy-odd year old, sprawling greenhouse set in the middle of an island park. Neither of them was interested in plants.

"Can you get rid of it?"

"I can't. I already love him."

"How do you know it's a boy?"

"I just do. A mother knows those things."

He thought about how young she looked, how impossible it seemed that she was talking about the things mothers knew. And he remembered that when they'd met he thought she looked like Cher, only prettier. He still thought that.

"You could give him away."

Quietly, they passed a collection of palm trees so tall they almost touched the glass dome above them. On the ground below was a collection of tropical plants. The whole place was green and warm and impossibly humid. Through the window they could see that it was already cold outside and the natural plants were dying out for the season.

Uncomfortable with the silence, the young man said, "Don't you think it's weird, looking at palm trees when Canada's just across the river?"

"Canada's always been there. And the whole point of this place is that the plants don't belong here."

"If I knew you better, I'd have known you'd say that."

"I have to tell my family you're going to do the right thing. You know what they'll be like if you don't."

"You're threatening me?"

"I'm telling you the truth. You know I am."

"You can't think of another way out of this?"

"You mean one where you don't have to do anything?"

"I mean one that doesn't wreck both our lives."

She frowned at him, like he'd said something stupid. "Nobody's life is getting wrecked. We're just having a baby."

"Why do you even want a baby?"

"Because when you have a baby there's always someone in the world who loves you. Who doesn't want that?"

He hesitated for a moment, and then said, "I think I could always love you."

"Then everything's perfect."

CHAPTER ONE

September 13, 1996
Friday night

Thelma Houston, Gloria Gaynor, Chic, The Bee Gees, Bette Midler's *Divine Miss M*. Junior had put them all and more onto two mixtapes, which were blaring out of our new Pioneer component stereo system. That, and a Jello mold, had been his contribution to our housewarming party. Well, there were also the striped bell-bottom pants he'd chosen to wear.

"What was he thinking?" my much younger, much prettier partner, Ronnie, asked after he'd dragged me into our newly painted deep-green home office. I was leaning on our partners desk. The party had begun an hour before at seven and had just been highjacked by our former roommate and now tenant, Junior Clybourne. "I never said anything about a seventies theme. Who has a themed housewarming party? It's about how pretty our kitchen is, not the freaking nineteen seventies."

The apartment was full of friends and clients, mostly Ronnie's, though my boss, Lydia Gonzalez, was there with her husband, Dwayne.

"And why did he bring food?" Ronnie went on. "I told him we had it handled."

"I'm sure he's just trying to be nice."

"A Jello mold? A Jello mold is nice?"

A Jello mold was also more sixties than seventies, but I decided not to bring that up since it wasn't a themed party anyway. "At least it's not the kind with olives and Spam."

"What? Olives? Spam—oh God, that's disgusting! Why would anyone...? Don't tell me. I don't want to know."

"It's a great party. People are having fun. Everyone loves the apartment."

"Condo."

"Co-op. Don't count your chickens," I said. The building was currently a co-op, though Ronnie had every intention of getting on the board and taking it condo, which would very nearly double its value. We'd lived there nearly a month, part of me was surprised he hadn't done it already.

"So, who's the kid?" he asked in a gossipy voice.

"What kid?"

"The one in living room hovering by the ficus."

"You don't know him? I assumed you—"

"No clue."

"Well, I don't know him.

"You're sure?"

With a leer, I asked, "Are you afraid I'm going to leave you for a younger man?"

"Always."

He wasn't. He knew how much I loved him. He'd just taken to teasing me about our age difference and how he was getting 'too old' for me.

"In that case, I'd better get out there and introduce myself."

I kissed Ronnie and then kissed him again. Part of me didn't want to leave that moment. I pulled myself away and walked out of the office. In the dining room, Ronnie's friend Doug, whose commitment ceremony we'd gone to at the end of July, waylaid me.

"This place is amazing. I love these old Spanish buildings. This is a George Riddle, right?"

"Maybe? Ronnie's the one who knows those things."

"I think our house was designed by an architect who worked with him. Or for him? I haven't been able to prove anything, but I'm sure of it."

Out of the corner of my eye, I saw Junior doing some disco moves. I decided I had to get as far away from him as possible, so I said, "Ronnie's down the hall in the office. Maybe he's got some ideas on how you can find out."

I squeezed Doug's upper arm—I noticed he'd been going to the gym —and moved on. When I was back in the living room, the boy was still there by the ficus. Alone. It seemed odd that he was alone.

Wearing a pair of baggy jeans and an over-sized tomato red hoodie. He was young, small, and had a shock of black hair hanging over his left eye. His skin was dark enough to make me wonder if he was Mexican, and he hadn't quite learned the art of shaving. But that wouldn't explain his standing alone; a lot of our guests were at least part Mexican-American and several spoke Spanish. If he crossed the border yesterday he would still be welcome in this room.

So why did he look so lost?

I was halfway across the room when Lydia stopped me. "Meeting Tuesday afternoon. There are a couple of cases Edwin and I are considering taking on. We'd like your input."

"No business," Dwayne said. "You promised."

Ignoring him, she added, "And Dickie Keswick says 'Hi'."

"How exciting," I grumbled. "Tell Dickie to fuck off."

"Here, here," Dwayne agreed.

I didn't know what Dwayne's problem with Dickie was, but I certainly didn't need to hear from the guy. I'd let him interview me for a book he wrote about a member of the Chicago Outfit and I'd been sorry about it ever since.

"Don't be like that," Lydia said to me, seeming not to care about her husband's opinion. "He wants to do a book on Danny Osborne. Which I think would be good for Danny, he's been struggling since his release. You and Dickie may have to spend some time together."

"I can't tell you how excited I am." I said, mostly because I wasn't.

She was frowning at me and I doubted the conversation would improve, so it seemed a good time to slip away. The boy was only a few feet away, so I basically turned to him and said, "Hi. I'm Dom Reilly and you are?"

He looked at me for a long moment, and then said, "I'm Cass Reilly. You're my dad."

I suspected my heart stopped though I wasn't sure. My breathing definitely did. I knew exactly who he was. After I bought Dom Reilly's identi-fication, I took at trip out to Detroit to make sure no one was looking for him. In the process, I spent some time sitting in front of the apartment building where the real Dom Reilly had lived with his pretty young wife and little boy of about four.

I remembered that I'd seen her walking the boy from the building to a waiting Cadillac. This was that little boy. Same black hair, dark eyes and button nose. Wary expression.

My heart started again and I knew I had to get him out of there. The only person who might have heard what he said was Lydia—well, maybe Dwayne. She already knew I wasn't Dom Reilly and that this wasn't my kid. Lord knows what Dwayne knew.

I grabbed the kid by the upper arm and hustled him out of the front door. We were on the stairs walking down to the courtyard, when he came out of shock and tried to pull away. "I can walk."

But I didn't let go until we were in the courtyard near the sidewalk at the front of the building. The sun had set an hour before and the court-yard lights had come on to show off our landscaping. There were benches in the back where we might have been more comfortable, but I didn't budge. Keeping my voice low, I said, "I'm not your father."

"Dominick Patrick Reilly, born at six-fourteen in the morning on February 13, 1954 at Detroit Memorial. Your father's name was Patrick Reilly and your mother was Verna Keith. My grandpa and grandma. They died six years after you ran off, by the way, within twenty-four hours of each other. They couldn't live without each other. I thought it sucked, but everyone said it was sweet. Romantic. Your Social Security number—"

"You can stop."

I stood there trying to decide what to do. It occurred to me I could just go along and say, 'Ooops, you got me. I'm your dad. Now go away,' but I knew that wouldn't work. First, I doubted he would go away. And second, I couldn't have him around my friends because he didn't fit the stories I'd told. In my made-up biography, I left Michigan when I was twenty and never looked back. That was before this kid was born. I tell people I was married to a woman once, so I guess it's possible I could have a kid by my imaginary wife, but he or she would be much younger than this boy. No, there was no way out of this without getting tangled up in my own barbed lies.

"I'm not your dad," I said, again. It was the truth, and I hoped he'd accept it and go away.

"You are. You married Joanne Di Stefano on November 19, 1978. I was born five months later."

"So you're what? Seventeen? Does your mother know you're here?"

He avoided that question—which told me she didn't know—and asked his own, "You're a gay? Is that why you left me and my mom?"

The party was still going on above us. It was now raining men loud enough that I didn't think anyone could hear our conversation, but I didn't want to find out I was wrong. I took the kid by the arm again and led him out onto the street. Then I steered him across Cherry Avenue to Bixby Park.

Less than a minute later we were in the park. We weren't too far from a streetlight and a sign that told us we couldn't legally drive around the park more than three times. At some point, it had a been an active pick-up spot. Might still be. Street signs didn't always work.

"How did you find me?"

"Credit report."

"Credit report? You're a seventeen-year-old kid with access to people's credit reports?"

When I was a PI in Chicago, I had a contact in the credit department at Carson Pirie Scott who'd run reports for me. I doubted this kid was that clever.

He looked like he didn't want to tell me so I prompted him. "Come on, how did you get my credit report?"

"My mom works for this lawyer. He does collections. He buys people's debt, and then she calls them up and makes them pay. I have to pay room and board, so I work there on weekends catching up the filing and stuff. I went on my mom's computer and ran the report. She can't remember her passwords so she writes them down on a Post-It and puts them in her desk drawer. It wasn't hard."

I thought about all the information he'd gotten from the report. My address first and foremost. He knew I owned the co-op with Ronnie and that we'd taken out a small mortgage of fifty thousand—at one of the two banks in California that will write a mortgage on a co-op—to redo the kitchen and bathroom. I had tried hard for a long time to keep anyone from having my information. Now I was out there. Now people could find me. Or, rather, they could find Dom Reilly. I'd thought his name would keep me safe. I'd been wrong.

"You know that's illegal. Running my credit report," I said.

"Most of the things people want to do are illegal."

"Speaking of illegal... Your mom charges you room and board at seventeen?"

"That's not illegal. She's teaching me responsibility. And it's more than you ever did."

"I'm not your father."

"Stop saying that," he said loudly enough that I was glad I'd pulled him into the park.

I had to tell him the truth. Or at least something like it. "I bought your father's information from a guy in Reno. Birth certificate, baptismal and confirmation certificates. High school diploma. And a Michigan driver's license which he kindly put my face on." I took a breath. I didn't really want to say this, but I had to. "I paid extra because he said your father was on the bottom of Lake Erie and wouldn't be using his identification."

For a brief moment he seemed to take it in, then reject it. "That's not true. You're lying. You're my dad."

"I was told he crossed someone in the Detroit mob. The Partnership."

"That's not true either. No one ever said anything about my dad being in the Mafia."

"I didn't say he was in it. I said he pissed someone off who was."

"That's not what happened."

"Okay. What do you remember?"

"Nothing. I was four."

"What have people told you?"

"My mother said he just left. She came home one day and he was gone. His stuff was gone. She's never heard from him again."

"Stuff includes his important papers?"

"I guess."

It was an important point. The documents I had were originals. And that meant that I very likely had the important papers Dom Reilly disappeared with. Or possibly, Dom Reilly disappeared and then someone got rid of the papers. Though that didn't explain how they got from Detroit to Reno.

I could see that Cass was making his own calculations, struggling to keep believing I was his father. I tried to nudge that along.

"Do I look like your father?"

"I told you, I don't remember."

"Your mother doesn't have pictures of your dad?"

"She was mad at him for running off, so she got rid of them."

"You've never seen a picture of your dad?"

"No, I have. I have other relatives. It's just been a long time."

He was looking closely at me. Trying to figure out if I actually looked like the pictures he'd seen somewhere a long time ago. My guess was I didn't since he was starting to crumble.

"He's not in Lake Erie. He can't be."

"He might not be. That's just what I was told."

The trouble was, if I was using his identity, living as him, then what *was* he doing? Who was he pretending to be? The most likely answer was no one.

"When was the last time you ate?"

"Breakfast. Eastern time."

That had to be fifteen, sixteen hours. A long time for a growing boy. "Come on," I told him and then led him across the park to the Park Pantry. When we got inside the restaurant, we were led to a teal-colored booth on the Broadway side. The waitress, whose sister worked the breakfast shift, put menus in front of us.

Cass didn't pick his menu up. He just sat there looking out the window. I scanned my menu, but I knew what I wanted: a chicken Caesar. I probably should have eaten more at the party. There was, after all, a ton of food sitting on my dining room table. But I was here and not there so I might as well eat.

"You really think he's dead?"

"I do."

"Shit."

CHAPTER TWO

C indy's sister came over to take our order. I couldn't remember her name because I mostly came to the diner for their excellent breakfast. She was shorter and wider than her sister but just as nice. I ordered my salad and an iced tea, then she turned to Cass.

He shook his head. "I don't want anything."

"He'll have a bacon burger, curly fries with ranch dressing, and a Coke."

"You got it," Cindy's sister said and then walked away.

"I told you I don't want anything."

"You don't have to eat it. I won't make you pay for it." That made me wonder, "How'd you get here?"

"You brought me."

"No. How'd you get from Detroit to Long Beach?"

"Airplane."

Since I doubted he'd been keeping an eye out for cheap flights, I suspected that had been spontaneous and had cost a bundle.

"How'd you pay for it?"

"Credit card."

"You steal your mother's card?"

He was saved by Cindy's sister delivering our drinks. She said, "I forgot to ask. How did you want that burger?"

"Medium rare."

"Well," Cass corrected me.

When she left, I waited for Cass to answer my question. He didn't. "Does your mother know where you are?"

"She's in Sault Sainte Marie."

I'd heard of it but couldn't tell you where it was. "What's she doing there?"

"Casino."

His answers were not exactly explanatory. My guess was he hadn't told her where he was. And that she didn't exactly care. I was also getting the impression she wasn't exactly careful with money.

Those were his problems though. I needed to figure out mine. "So are you going to give me trouble?"

"What do you mean?"

"I like being Dom Reilly. I'd like to keep being Dom Reilly."

"What you're doing's illegal, isn't it?"

"Probably. I haven't bothered to check, but I'd guess there are at least half dozen laws I'm breaking."

I had a feeling about where this was going. I was about to be asked for child support of some sort. Also known as blackmail.

"I overheard people talking at the party. Are you some kind of cop?"

"I'm an investigator for a lawyer. I was a cop, a long time ago, but no one knows that."

"Who do you think killed my dad?"

"No idea."

We sat there for a bit not saying anything. Mostly I think we were figuring out what we wanted from each other. Our meal came. He took a bite of the burger right away. I ate some salad.

He swallowed, and said, "If you find out who killed my dad then you can keep being him."

"There's a little problem with that. If we find who killed your dad and you turn them in to the police, I can't be Dom Reilly anymore."

"I'm not going to turn them in. I'm going to kill them." Then he took a bigger bite of his burger, pushed in a couple of French fries after it, and guzzled some Coke. The idea of murdering a murderer seemed to have improved his appetite.

I should not do this. That was my first thought. But if I didn't the kid could, and probably would, throw a grenade into my life and that would be it. I wouldn't be able to be Dom Reilly. And I couldn't go back to being Nick Nowak. I'd be nobody. I'd lose the life I probably shouldn't have built in the first place. The life I loved. I wondered if it was too late to lie to the kid and tell him I really was his dad. Maybe I could make that work.

No. I couldn't.

"Okay, sure. I'll help you find out who killed your dad."

He'd over-filled his mouth and was chewing hard. Still, he managed to smile.

"You go back home. I'll go to Reno in a week or so and try to find the guy who sold me your dad's papers. Get him to tell me who he bought them from and we'll go from there."

He swallowed hard. "No. We need to do it now."

"What's the hurry?"

He'd taken another bite though and I had to wait. "I don't trust you," he said with his mouth still half full. Teenagers were meant to be innocent and a little gullible. I wondered what happened to this one to make him so cagey.

"Okay, we'll go to Reno tomorrow. First thing."

He shook his head. "Can we drive there?"

"It's an eight- or nine-hour trip. We wouldn't get there until tomorrow morning."

"Let's go to the airport."

I didn't like that. I dug into my salad so I could think it through. He wanted to go to the airport *now*. While there was a party going on at my apartment. Going back to grab a few things wasn't going to be easy. In fact, it was going to be impossible. Ronnie would flip out that I was leaving. Rightfully so. I'd have to explain who the kid was, truthfully or not, and why we had to leave right this minute—again, truthfully or not. All of that was challenging. Too challenging.

"You didn't bring anything with you? Luggage?" I asked.

"I have a backpack. I put it in the bushes in front of your place."

This was definitely sounding very fly-by-night on his part. Like he'd run the credit report, and then the first chance he got, stole his mother's credit card, and ran to the airport. And it didn't seem like he was going to slow down any time soon.

I'd finished the chicken part of my chicken Caesar. They did it differently at the Pantry, they breaded and deep fried a chicken breast, sliced it, and plunked it on top of the salad. Their idea of health food, I guess.

Once I was done with the chicken I wasn't much interested in the lettuce below. Cass was finished with his burger and most of the way through his fries.

"Is it just Cass or is that short for something?"

"Cassidy. My mother loved David Cassidy."

David wouldn't have been a bad choice if you were naming a kid after the teen idol. Which made me wonder, "How old was your mom when you were born?"

"Seventeen."

"That's young."

He shrugged. He'd probably heard that before. But it was true. He was seventeen and I didn't think he could be trusted with a credit card, no less a baby. Cindy's sister came over and asked if we wanted anything else. I asked for the check.

"What were you expecting?" I asked, once she was gone. "Did you think you'd just show up at your dad's place and he'd be all excited to see you?"

"Maybe."

Not very clear. It suddenly occurred to me that he might have wanted money from his dad. Love, revenge, money. The big motivators.

"Do you need money?"

"Not really. My mom does okay. And I'm gonna get a full-time job. When I graduate high school."

That left love and revenge.

"Were you mad at your dad? Did you want to tell him that?"

"A little, maybe. I think I just wanted to know, like, why did he leave?"

So it was love. He wanted to know why he didn't get the love he deserved. That's why he was so fast to switch to killing the person who murdered his dad. They'd taken that away from him.

Cindy's sister brought the check. I left a generous tip on the table and we went up to the register to pay. As we were walking across the park on the way back to my apartment, the kid asked, "So the guy who sold you my dad's stuff. You don't have his phone number?"

"I don't have his last name. He was called Gavin. That's all I know. Basically the guy's a forger. You don't put people like that in your address book."

"How are we going to find him?"

"I know a place to ask for him." I explained, "I was working in this bar under the table a couple days a week. Some kids came in who looked way too young to drink. I asked for ID and they showed it to me. It was good, very good—but I still didn't believe they were in their twenties. I offered them free drinks if they told me who made their IDs. That's how I heard about Gavin. They said he kept 'business hours' at a casino called Hobart's in North Valley. I went to see him a couple of days later. Couple days after that I went to his place and picked everything up."

"So you *do* know where he lives?"

"I'm not sure I can find it again."

We were nearly in front of my building, El Matador, stopping right by the sign. I could hear the party going on above. Cass went to get his backpack. It was still before nine so I shouldn't have been surprised when John Gallagher walked up with this guy, Melvin, who he'd been dating for a few weeks.

Like Junior, John had been our roommate and was now our tenant. He was tall and thin with tightly curled blond hair. Melvin was shaped like a fire hydrant. John wore short jean cut-offs, a mesh shirt and roller skates. Melvin looked like the leather guy in The Village People and held a casserole in his hands.

"What are you doing out here?" John asked.

"I've had kind of an emergency. Don't tell Ronnie you saw me."

"Are you some kind of doctor?" Melvin asked.

"It's a personal emergency," I said. "You know the party isn't seventies themed?"

"I'm going to kill Junior."

"I'm scared to ask what that is," I said, indicating the casserole.

"Velveeta surprise," John said. Then to Melvin, "Maybe we should put it in the car."

"You drove?" I asked. The house we rented to him and Junior was within walking distance.

"We were at Melvin's."

And then Cass was back with his backpack slung over one shoulder. Immediately, John was curious. "And who is this?"

"We have to go," I said. "Enjoy the party. And if Ronnie seems upset, tell him I'm going to call him in a couple hours. Thanks."

And then I pushed Cass down the street toward my Jeep. My 1994 Wrangler was half a block down 1st Street. Most of the Jeep was Forest Green. I'd been sideswiped, so pretty much everything on the left side had been repainted. It had looked perfect when I picked it up, but a month later it had settled into a darker green than the rest of the vehicle. Ronnie kept telling me to take it back and complain.

Of course, I didn't have my keys. They were sitting in a bowl on the bedroom dresser upstairs. I walked around to the passenger side and reached under, directly below the word JEEP. I felt around until I found the magnetic key box. Most people keep them in a wheel well. I felt like this was the kind of thing that required a bit of originality. I popped it open and there was my spare key. We were set to go.

Once inside, I said, "You realize this is somewhere between blackmail and kidnapping."

"Do you want to call the cops?"

I did not.

CHAPTER THREE

September 13, 1996
Still later

Even though it was a Friday night, freeway traffic was light and we made it to the airport about nine-twenty. Cass had fallen asleep before we got to the 710. Not surprising. It was around midnight in Michigan and I had the impression he'd gotten up very early that morning. At the airport, I parked in long-term parking, Lot B, and woke him up so we could catch the shuttle.

It showed up a few minutes after we got to the stop. I made a mental note that my car was somewhere around the C6 marker. Since I had no idea what airline we should take, I asked the driver. "We want to fly to Reno, any idea which airline we should take?"

She was a nice Black lady who looked at me with amusement and said, "How about Reno Air? Terminal 4."

"That'll work. Thanks."

Cass looked groggy, but I felt like I should make conversation. "Have you flown a lot?"

"Yeah. My mom used to take me places."

He was a more experienced traveler than I was then. I'd only flown a couple of times, once to Vegas and another time back to Detroit to check out Dom Reilly. I wasn't what you'd call a traveler. When I lived in Chicago there didn't seem much point, everything was there. Yeah, some people have to get away from the winter, but I was always fine with it. And Ronnie's not much of a traveler, either. We've been to Palm Springs, Rosarito and Santa Barbara together. The second two were only because we were loaned vacation houses by his clients. He was not the sort to spend thousands of dollars on anything that wasn't either tax deductible or likely to return his investment twofold.

We reached terminal 4 and found the Reno Air ticket counter. There was a flight at 10:10 we could just make. After she sold us the tickets and took our names, the girl said, "Father and son? I can see the resemblance."

"Adopted," Cass said, which saved me from telling her she needed to have her glasses checked.

"Well... people grow together. No luggage?"

Fortunately, there wasn't much of a line at security. Unfortunately, when I walked through the scanner it went off. I wasn't surprised. I had a lot of hardware holding my shoulder blade together. I explained this to the security guard as he ran a wand over me. Since the wand went off exactly where I said it would he let me through.

Of course the gate was at the far end of the terminal so we had to run most of the way. We made it onto the flight just before they closed the door. Our seats were 14A and 14B. There were probably twenty-some rows, two one side, three on the other. The plane was less than a quarter full. Which I guess was not a surprise. If you wanted to go to Reno for the weekend you'd have left hours ago.

I was getting edgy, not about flying but about Ronnie. I'd hoped there would be time to call him before we left. The flight was going to be around an hour and a half. That meant I wouldn't be able to call him until close to midnight. I told myself the party would still be going so I should just relax. Plus, there wasn't anything I could do about it.

The stewardess taught us how to buckle a safety belt, and explained that the flight was too short for meal service but there would be drinks and snacks coming around once we were in the air. Then the seatbelt light went on and we were speeding down the runway.

The plane rose at a steep and uncomfortable pitch. The planes I'd flown on before had been much larger, with two aisles and at least eight seats across. They seemed to lumber into the air, approaching everything gradually and much more gently. This smaller plane jumped into the air and sped upwards.

I wasn't liking it. Cass, though, seemed untroubled. He sat next to the window looking out at the receding lights of Los Angeles. There was awe on his face. He seemed so young. I wondered if he really understood what it meant to kill someone. I didn't doubt he knew what it meant to *want* to kill someone, but that was different from actually doing it. When we found his father's killer, he believed he was going to want to kill them. I didn't think he'd be able to.

Soon, the plane leveled off, and the stewardess' got the drinks cart out and began coming down the aisle. I leaned a bit closer to Cass, and said, "Tell me everything you know about your father."

"I just know he disappeared."

"You know more than that. You said you were born four months after your parents got married. So they had to get married."

"I guess."

"And your mom was seventeen and your dad was twenty-four, twenty-five—do I have that right?"

"Yeah."

"So, where did they meet? Did your mother ever say? It wouldn't have been in school, unless your dad was a teacher. And it wouldn't have been some place teenagers are supposed to be, would it?"

"They met at Harpo's. It was a disco then with this floor that had lights underneath. I saw Napalm Death there last summer."

I had no idea what Napalm Death was, but it had to be weird to see them at the place your parents met. "Your mother was there underage."

"She and her best friend, Heather, used to get in everywhere just because they were pretty and had cool clothes. That's what my mother says, anyway."

"Do you know anything else about the night they met?"

"They Hustled. You know, the disco dance. My mom told him she was nineteen."

"She told you that she lied?"

"No. My grandparents told me that part."

Lying is not a great foundation for a relationship. Though I wasn't one to talk. Ronnie didn't know my real age, which was four years older than he thought.

The drinks cart arrived and the stewardess asked if we'd like a beverage. Cass order a ginger ale and I said, "Me too." She gave us the drinks and a small package of nuts each, and then moved on.

"Are you an alcoholic?" Cass asked.

"No. I just don't drink much."

Drinking loosened my tongue and I had too many secrets for a loose tongue. Of course, not liking your behavior when you drink was one of the many definitions of alcoholism. But we won't think about that.

Pouring my ginger ale, I asked, "Did your parents date for long before they got married?"

"Four months. I mean, you can count, right?"

"Four months? Or, at *least* four months? Did she get pregnant the night they met?"

"How would I know?"

"What have people said?" I had to remind him.

He thought for a moment, chewing on a nut, then said, "One time she said I was premature and my grandmother snorted."

"Your mother's mother or your father's mother."

"My Grandma D."

That must be D for Di Stefano.

"What difference does it make?" he demanded.

"I don't know that it makes any difference. When you're trying to figure something out you just ask a lot of questions until you get some answers. What do people say their marriage was like?"

"Um... my grandma and grandpa never liked my mother. I remember that. There was always a fight when they wanted to see me. Which kinda ruined birthdays and stuff."

"Do you have any idea *why* they never liked her?"

He shrugged, ate another nut. "I think I remember her saying she was too much for them."

"What does 'too much' mean?"

"She likes to have fun, play cards, wear cool clothes."

"She never remarried?"

"She's still married to my dad."

"There are ways to divorce a husband you can't find."

"She didn't do that."

"Boyfriends?"

He didn't answer right away. He'd finished his nuts so he crumpled up the package. I hadn't touched mine so I put my package onto his tray. I sipped my ginger ale and waited. Finally, he said, "She has a lot of friends."

I took that to mean she had men in her life, just none that were permanent. He was starting to get touchy about her, though, so I decided to go in a different direction. "Your father disappeared in 1982 when you were four. I bought his papers in Reno in 1986. I suppose it's possible that he was living under a different name and decided to sell his old identity."

"So, he could still be alive?" Cass said. The hope in his voice made me cringe.

"Possible but not likely."

"You disappeared and no one knows where you are."

That wasn't exactly true. Some people knew exactly where I was. I didn't go into it though.

"Why can't you be who you really are?" Cass asked.

"The mob is sort of after me." It was the truth but it sounded kind of ridiculous.

"Why aren't you in witness protection?"

"I'm kind of doing that on my own. Plus I'm wanted by the police for murder. I think."

"You're not sure? That's stupid. How can you not be sure?"

"It was a long time ago. And now they have DNA so maybe they figured out I wasn't even there. It's not like they can call me." We needed to not be talking about me. "Look, there are reasons I disappeared. Not really your business, okay? Do you know if your dad had reasons?"

"I guess he didn't like my mom."

"That's a reason to get divorced not a reason to disappear. And most people who disappear don't ditch their identities. They move far away and don't list their telephone number. They might not file taxes for a while, but that only matters if you've broken the law. If you haven't broken the law the IRS can't give your address to just anyone so they probably file. Do you know if anyone filed a missing person report on your dad?"

"I'm not sure, but I don't think so."

"Everyone thinks he ran off on his own?"

"No one talks about it."

"If someone murdered your dad—and I think that's probably what happened—then they either went to your house when you and your mom weren't there and took all of his stuff, or your mom knows what happened and she got rid of all his stuff."

I let that sink in. I was careful not to say his mom killed his dad, though I was already leaning in that direction. I didn't want to push it, though. It would be better if Gavin told the kid it was his mom who sold him the papers. Cass could make his own connections.

A stewardess came down the aisle picking up the trash. I was pretty sure we'd be landing soon.

"You said your mom used to take you places. Where would she take you?"

"Atlantic City. Las Vegas. Places like that."

"Reno?"

"I don't remember."

That might be true. He might not remember. He would have been somewhere between four and eight. She could have come out at any time and sold the papers to Gavin. Neither of us said anything for a few minutes. I was thinking about the possibility his mother had something to do with his father's death. I wasn't sure whether he was thinking the same thing. On the upside, if his mother did kill his father then he probably wouldn't kill her.

Probably.

I decided to come at this from another direction. "So, why were you looking for you dad in the first place?"

"He's my dad."

"If you had found him, what were you expecting?"

"You asked me that all ready."

"Maybe I'm hoping for a better answer. Do you have one?"

He looked out the window for long enough that I wondered if he was going to say anything. Then he said, "I guess, that he'd be my dad again."

"You know... parents can be pretty disappointing even when they don't run off."

He shrugged. "But if he hadn't disappeared, I'd know if he was a good dad or not, wouldn't I?"

"You ran a credit report on your dad. Was this the first time?"

"No. I did it once last year."

Behind my back, Ronnie had gotten a couple credit cards for us both.

To build my credit. I didn't know exactly when he'd done that, but those might have shown up.

"Were there a couple of credit cards on there?"

"Yeah. And an address in Long Beach. Not the one you have now. A different one."

"Why didn't you come last year?"

"I wasn't sure. I thought my mom might have taken them out."

"What made you think that?"

"She did it before. Eighty-seven, eighty-eight. She took out some cards, had them sent to a guy she knows up in Traverse who gave them to her, and then ran the cards up and never paid for them." He gave me a funny look and asked, "You never wondered why your credit sucked?"

"I didn't use it so I never thought about it."

But, now that I *was* thinking about it, Ronnie had access to credit reports. He'd have seen those cards from eighty-seven, eighty-eight. He must have known there was something funny about them—especially if they went to an address in Traverse, wherever that was. The story I'd told him, the story I told everyone, was that I was living with my wife in the valley in the eighties—not in Michigan. But there was nothing on my credit report that would support my story. I was surprised Ronnie never brought it up.

And then we began the steep descent into Reno-Tahoe International Airport. It was the kind of landing that those in the airline industry describe as smooth and those of us who are passengers wonder if we should send them a dictionary. For a few terrifying moments I wondered if the plane might break apart and fly away in different directions. Luckily, it didn't.

When we came off the plane, there was a small group of people waiting to pick up their relatives. There was no one waiting for us. We were at gate C4. We weren't very far down the concourse when I saw a bank of pay phones. Across from the telephones there were two slot machines, but they didn't seem to be on. I gave the kid a twenty, and said, "See if you can find a newsstand that has any aspirin or Tylenol."

He gave me a questioning look but didn't ask. About six weeks before I'd had surgery on my shoulder. I'd gotten stiff on the plane ride even though it was less than ninety minutes. I took out a calling card and called our house phone. It was ten minutes before midnight.

Ronnie answered, "Hello."

I didn't say anything for too long a time.

"I know it's you, Dom."

"I'm sorry. Something's come up and I have to deal with it."

"So, who's the kid?"

"His dad is someone I used to know."

"Where are you?"

"Reno." Well, he would get the credit card statement, which meant he'd find out anyway.

"Does this have anything to do with the people you were with at the Westin a few weeks ago?"

Okay, I didn't know he knew about that. My friends Brian and Sugar had come through from Chicago on their way to a Mexican cruise. I'd met them for a drink in the lobby of the Westin Hotel. We'd spend all of thirty-five minutes together and it had gotten back to him. Which didn't surprise me but also didn't make me happy.

"No, it has nothing to do with that."

"What does it have to do with?"

"The kid's father is missing. I said I'd help him figure out what happened to him."

"And that had to happen in the middle of our housewarming party?"

"It did."

He left the kind of silence that shouted 'I don't believe you.'

"When will you be back?"

"Soon. I hope."

"You can't be more specific?"

"No."

We left another long pause.

"I don't want to be doing this," I said.

"But you are."

CHAPTER FOUR

September 13, 1996
Very late

Fortunately, I always carried a couple of hundred-dollar bills in the 'secret' compartment of my wallet. It's not that I was walking through life expecting to be quasi-kidnapped by a teenager; it's more that I knew bad things happened and that bad things generally required cash.

Once we got out of the terminal, I was hit by the frigid air, clearly under fifty degrees. I was wearing a pair of 501s, Vans and a thin red turtleneck Ronnie had picked out. I usually left a jacket in my Jeep, but Ronnie had cleaned everything out when it went to the body shop to be fixed. Not many of my things had worked their way back in.

Unlike LAX and other big city airports, there were not a lot of cabs waiting for us. In fact there were none. I walked down to a recent model minivan that had its windows open and was sitting there idling. The main clue that it might be for hire was that it was illegally parked.

I leaned in and asked "Are you looking for a fare?"

The guy inside was in his twenties, ill-kept, and scrawny. He was trying to hide a joint in one hand, but the smell of the vehicle gave him away.

"Oh yeah, man. You wanna go someplace?"

I glanced around the airport and if there'd been another option I would have taken it. Instead, I pulled out my wallet. Snagged a hundred-dollar bill from the 'secret' compartment and held it up so the guy could see it.

"You busy for the next two hours?"

"I am now."

Cass and I climbed into the backseat. He'd been trying to hand me a bag with aspirin since I'd hung up the phone. I was unhappy about the call and distracted so I hadn't really noticed. I did now. As I opened the bag I said to the driver, "First we want to go to Hobart's. You know it?"

As he pulled away from the curb he said, "Yeah. Why you wanna go there, man? It's a pretty sleazy place."

"I guess it hasn't changed much then."

"Oh yeah, you been before?"

"Yeah. I've been here before."

He shrugged. "You know what you're doing."

"We won't be there long." I'd gotten a couple of Bayer aspirins out of the metal travel box and popped them in my mouth. I chewed them up and swallowed them. Disgusting, but that's how much my shoulder hurt.

"So where you from?" our driver asked.

"Out of town," I said with as much finality as I could muster.

"Oh right... yeah... I'll just..." He reached over and turned on the radio. The "Macarena" was playing, which was annoying. At that particular moment it seemed to be playing everywhere.

I looked over at Cass. He was staring out the window as the airport slipped away. He was forlorn, as they say. I had to be honest with myself. It wasn't likely we'd find Gavin, and if we did find him there was no guarantee he'd remember where he got Dom Reilly's important papers. But the best way to get this forlorn kid to give up would be going on a wild goose chase.

Our driver was singing along to the "Macarena" except he didn't know the words. It was working my nerves, so I asked, "What's your name?"

"Spencer."

"Thanks for driving us Spencer. So you seem like a guy who might be connected. You mind if I ask you a few questions?"

"There aren't any legal brothels in Reno. Everyone comes here thinking there are, but you have to go out into the boonies. You might find some girls working Hobarts, but they're not legal so you have to be careful."

"Thanks. You hear much about where I could get a fake ID?" I asked.

"For your..." He didn't know what Cass was to me so he stopped. "Um, there's a bartender named Philly at Hobart's, he might know."

"Do you know where I can get a gun?" Cass asked.

"Don't answer that," I said. "It's a joke."

I stared at Cass during an awkward pause, which was eventually broken by Spencer. "What hotel you staying at? Cause I know people at Circus Circus, you'd like it there. I could maybe get you a discount."

"Thanks Spencer, we'll keep that in mind."

The idea of checking into a hotel and going to sleep was the furthest thing from my mind. The kid wanted a gun. I had to figure out how to dissuade him from killing another human being while at the same time figuring out who that human being might be.

Hobart's Casino sat in the middle of a large parking lot. There was a half-hearted attempt at a mining theme on the outside with a pick axe and a gold pan above the automatic sliding doors at the front.

"So if you'll just wait here, Spencer, I won't be long." I began to slide the door open but noticed that Cass was scooting over to come with me. "Where do you think you're going?"

"I'm coming with you."

"You're not old enough to be in a casino."

In the front seat, Spencer nodded, as though he'd just gotten the answer to why I might want a fake ID.

"I've been in casinos before."

I knew they might not have a problem with his being there as long as he didn't try to gamble, but I wanted him to stay in the parking lot. Particularly if he was going to ask more people where to get a gun or otherwise plan a murder.

"Yeah, I don't need you getting me thrown out in the middle of a conversation. I'll be back in ten minutes." Then I shut the van door in his face.

His surprised and angry look amused me as I turned around and walked into the casino. I was immediately hit by a wall of cigarette smoke. I'd quit years ago, and while I sometimes missed it, it had grown disgusting. I knew if I went back to it now it would take several packs until I could get to the point of enjoying it again. It was no longer tempting.

The carpet was red and gold with bucking horses trying to throw cowboys off. Along one side of the large space there were banks of slot machines. Down the center were the tables, a whole section was roped off due to the time of night. A couple were actually full though. They had one dollar blackjack, which looked to be as popular as it was in Las Vegas. On the far side of the room, there was a long oval shaped bar with video poker machines set into it every few feet.

I walked over to the bar and got the attention of a barmaid who was dressed in a red uniform that matched the carpet and might have been 'Western' if they'd had miniskirts in the Wild West.

"Hi. I'm looking for a guy named Gavin."

She shrugged.

"What about a bartender named Philly?"

"He's the bald guy at the other end of the bar," she said, then sipped from a glass of what looked like Coke but was probably rum and Coke.

I nodded and walked down the long bar. She was right, he was pretty bald, though he stubbornly combed a couple of extra-long strands of hair from the sides over the top. He was smoking a cigarette, which went a long way to explain his gray skin and broken capillaries.

"I'm looking for Gavin," I said, without introduction.

"Who are you?"

"Former client."

He looked me up and down, then said, "He's not doing returns. He's in prison last I heard."

"Why's he in prison?"

"If you're a former client then you know why."

I nodded. Forgery. It was one of those crimes that might have sent him to prison for a short time or a very long time—depending on how many times they could prove it. I had no way of knowing how long his sentence had been. It was possible he might be out already. It wouldn't be surprising if he decided not to jump back into his former profession.

"You don't happen to know which prison?"

"We're not pen pals."

"Sure. I went to his place once. It was a single-wide but it wasn't in a park. You know where that might be?"

"Sun Valley, maybe. 5th Avenue. 6th."

"You know if anyone took over his business?"

"Someone probably did, but they don't come in here."

Which made me wonder if the casino had something to do with his getting busted. That had nothing to do with me so I let it go.

"Thanks for answering my questions," I said. I dropped a twenty on the bar and walked out of the casino.

Back in the minivan, Cass was pissed off and surly. "What did you find out?"

"We're going down to Sun Valley. I'm looking for a single wide on 5th or 6th."

"Okay," Spencer said doubtfully. "There's probably more than one."

"I've been there before. I'm hoping I recognize it when I see it."

Spencer started the van and pulled out of the casino's parking lot.

"So he wasn't in there?" Cass asked.

"The bartender said he's in prison, but he doesn't know which one. He might be out or there might be someone at his place who knows."

"So we're not going to find out what we need to know tonight?"

"No. I don't think we are."

The thing was, I felt like we had figured it out. He admitted that his mother might have brought him to Reno after his father disappeared. In my mind, the *might* part of that sentence had already evaporated. His mother had brought him out to Reno while she sold his father's papers to Gavin, and then gambled the money away. Or she might have won. It didn't matter if she walked away with most of the money or not. The point was, she sold her husband's important papers. She knew he wasn't coming back. She knew he was dead. And she probably knew who killed him. That is, if she didn't do it herself.

It took less than ten minutes to get to the Sun Valley area. We pulled into the neighborhood. I looked for something familiar but didn't see it. I tried to think of the color the trailer had been. Nothing came to mind. That told me something though. It wasn't an unusual or remarkable color. I would have remembered orange, red, bright blue, bright yellow—bright anything. Pink, lime green, black. That left gray, light yellow, light blue, white, beige. All the super bland colors. All the colors trailers actually were.

We drove up and down 5th and 6th Avenues twice. I was already beginning to think about what we should do next as we passed a white single-wide with gray shutters.

"Slow down," I said.

The chain-link fence was familiar, but then a lot of the homes on this street hand them. On one side of the yard there was a twenty-year-old Plymouth Duster sitting on blocks. It was army green. It had still been in use when I'd been there before. I remembered it because I'd owned a Plymouth Duster once. Mine had been baby blue.

"This is it."

Spencer came to a complete stop. There was a light on in what looked like the living room. Before I'd thought much about it, I jumped out of the van. I shut the door, but before I'd gotten all the way up the driveway the door opened and Cass was twenty feet behind me. I stopped.

"Go back to the van."

"Fuck you. This is about my father. I'm coming."

"I don't know if this is about anything, but I'd rather you stayed in the van."

"I'm the one in charge here."

I immediately regretted the comment I'd made earlier about blackmail and kidnapping. If I were being blackmailed or kidnapped, and it certainly felt like I was, then he *was* in charge and there wasn't a whole lot I could do about it.

The door to the trailer opened behind me. I turned and there was a woman of about thirty looking at us through a screen door. She said, "I have a gun."

"That's all right," I said. "You're not going to need it. We're not going to hurt you. I want to ask if you remember a guy named Gavin."

"Gavin was my dad."

"Was?"

"He died last year."

"In prison?"

She shook her head. "He had cancer so they let him out early. Mostly so they didn't have to pay for it. Did you know my dad?"

"Yeah, I met him a couple times. I came here once."

"You're not a friend then. So what do you want?"

"I wanted to talk to your dad about a woman who came to see him. It would have been sometime between eighty-three and eighty-six. Were you living here then?"

"Yeah, but I don't remember. I mean, most of the people who came around were teenagers or scary looking guys."

Cass chipped in, "She had long black hair then. Really pretty."

"She might have had a kid with her. Five, six... seven."

It was hard to see through the screen, but she might have been thinking it over. Finally she asked, "Purple leather coat?"

"Yeah, she has a purple coat," Cass said. His voice was flat, lifeless.

"I wanted that coat. My dad said he'd buy me one cause he was going to make a lot of money off her. But then he never did."

I could hear three decades of disappointment in that last sentence. Gavin probably did make a lot of money off Joanne Di Stefano. I paid five thousand. He likely paid her one, two at the most. I glanced at Cass. I had the feeling this was bad. He'd just gotten confirmation that his mother sold his father's identity, meaning she knew he was dead and might have, probably had, something to do with his death.

I thanked Gavin's daughter, who'd never given us her name, and walked down to the minivan with Cass. Once we were in the van, Spencer asked, "Where to now?"

I had no idea.

CHAPTER FIVE

September 14, 1996
Saturday, the wee hours

There were only two choices: get a hotel room and catch some sleep or go back to the airport and wait for a departing flight. It was nearly one o'clock. By the time we picked out a hotel and got a room it would be two. There'd be flights in just a few hours. I wanted to go home and send this kid on his way as soon as possible.

"Airport."

Spencer turned us around and drove for about a block before he said, "You haven't been here long. You sure you don't wanna stick around take in the sights? It's a great place. Lots to do and not just gambling. There's shows and great places to eat. Lots of buffets. There's, like, hiking and stuff. Nature, you know?"

"Yeah, we came on business," I said. "And we just concluded that business so I think we'd like to go. No offense to Reno."

"Hey, I'm just letting you know... It's a great place."

I didn't buy it. I looked over at Cass again. He was in shock. Part of me wanted to fix that, but it also seemed a good idea to let him stew in his juices.

The drive to the airport wasn't even ten minutes. It was late enough that Spencer was able to speed through the city, zipping through a couple of yellow lights that I would definitely have stopped at. We pulled up in front of the terminal about forty feet from where we'd found Spencer to begin with. As promised, I gave him a hundred-dollar bill.

"Thanks, man." As we climbed out of the van he added, "Enjoy the rest of your stay and your trip back to... you know, wherever."

Once we were inside the terminal, I realized I'd been so intent on getting to a pay phone when we landed that I'd barely looked around. The ticket area was under construction and half of it was covered by dingy tarps and scaffolding. The remaining ticket counters were squeezed together and their signage had been compressed into a much smaller space. None of the counters were open at that time of the morning.

Opposite the counters hung an electrified board that listed the flights. I went and stood in front of it. The first flight out to Detroit was United Airlines at 5:15. Reno Air had a flight back to Long Beach leaving at 6:10. My plan was that we'd be on separate flights.

"I think you should forget about this and just go home now," I said to Cass.

"No. I'm not going to forget about it."

"Look, Gavin told me your dad got in trouble with the mob and ended up in Lake Erie. He had to have been given that information by your mom."

"She never told me that."

"Well, she wouldn't, would she?"

"You don't know her."

"It makes sense, though. Your dad might not have been part of The Partnership, but he crossed someone who was. Your mom knows that, but what could she do? She wouldn't have gone to the police. That would have been dangerous. She'd be better off pretending your dad ran off, so she got rid of his stuff and sold his identity. It's best to leave this alone."

"You're wrong."

"Okay. What's your explanation?" There was a long pause while he tried to think of one. I waited. And waited. And I finally said, "You know, I think I'd like to find a men's room."

It had been a really long time since I'd taken a piss. I left the kid standing there. There was a wide hallway leading out to the gates. I could see the metal detector partway down. A bored looking security guard sat next to it. There were restrooms just before you had to go through security. I went in and took my time. Yeah, I needed to do my business, but I also had to think.

I'd just challenged the kid to come up with another explanation. Was he going to be able to? What would it be? And did he even care? Joanne Di Stefano knew her husband was dead. She'd told Gavin so.

Of course, she might have lied to make his papers more valuable. I'd paid five thousand because it was a life I could just step into. Okay, that hadn't worked out as well as I'd hoped. But still...

And maybe the real Dom Reilly *was* out there somewhere living a life he'd bought somewhere and just stepped into. It was possible. But the more I thought about it the more unlikely it seemed.

I washed my hands, threw some cold water on my face, and walked back out to the ticketing area. Outside on the sidewalk there were a couple of janitors smoking. Opposite the ticket area was baggage claim. A guy in a rumpled suit slept on one of the benches over there. A luggage carousel was turning though it held no luggage and wouldn't for hours.

Cass was standing under the arrivals and departures sign looking like he hadn't moved at all. I stood next to him and waited. After a bit, I said, "I'd like to go home and forget this whole thing. I think you should do the same."

"I have to know if she killed him."

"No, you don't. Has she been a good mother to you?"

"She a great mom."

The picture he'd painted of a flamboyant gambler wasn't of a classic great mom, but I didn't want to lose the advantage. "Then nothing else matters."

"Even if she killed him?"

"Maybe she was a great mom *because* she killed him. Maybe she's making it up to you."

It was a stretch, I know. Killer mom makes good. But he was just a kid and it might not be hard to put one over—

"That's bullshit."

"Okay, if she's a great mom then she couldn't have killed him. That's your answer."

"You're right. She didn't do it."

I felt a surge of relief. I'd be home by lunch. Ronnie would have clients in the afternoon. I'd be able to take a long nap and figure out how to fix things with him by the time he got home.

"I still need to know who killed him."

Ah, shit. I felt my afternoon nap slipping away.

"Do you have any idea how dangerous it might be trying to find out? Not only to you and me, but to your mom?"

"It's only going to be dangerous if you fuck up. Are you going to fuck up?"

"Not on purpose. But the way these things go... We don't know a lot about what happened to your dad. That means we don't know if we're fucking up or not."

"We're not going to talk to anyone in the mob. You feel better?"

"No. Sometimes just talking about the wrong people is enough to get you killed."

"You're smart enough to figure this out."

"That's flattering. But it's not true."

"I think it is. And it's up to me."

I walked away. I pulled the tin of Bayer aspirin out of my back pocket and returned to the men's room. My shoulder was screaming again, so I ran some water into my scooped hand and swallowed four aspirin. It was more pleasant than chewing them. I walked back out and just stood there for a while.

I should go back and tell the kid to fuck off. What could he really do to me anyway? Lots. He could do lots. He could call Ronnie and tell him I wasn't really Dom Reilly. Well, I think my boyfriend already had at least some idea that was true. Ronnie would help me. We'd have to get Dom Reilly's name off our co-op. That meant a quit claim and a refinanced mortgage—awkward since I think we'd just made the first payment. We probably couldn't get that done before Cass called the DMV and told them my license was a fraud. That would be bad. Definitely illegal and likely to have consequences. Who else could he call? The IRS. Social Security. Those would be even stickier.

I'd probably have to leave as soon as I signed a quit claim for Ronnie. Hell, I could tell him to sign it himself and not even go back. And then what? The kid could get Ronnie in trouble. The fact that I'd gotten a mortgage as someone I'm not was kind of a federal crime, and if they thought Ronnie knew about he'd be in a lot of trouble even if I were nowhere to be found. For a real estate agent to be accused of mortgage fraud or even suspected—well, that was definitely a career killer. Which meant he'd lose his boyfriend and his career in short order. I couldn't do it. I loved him too much for that. I was running out of options.

When I got back to the ticketing area there were still no agents. I picked the time off the arrivals and departures sign. It was almost two. We had about two more hours to wait before we could buy tickets to anywhere.

Cass had found a bench next to the start of the construction. He was sitting there just staring. I stood a bit away just watching him. I wished I was the kind of guy who could drag the kid into the men's room and drown him in a toilet. Then I could come out, leave the terminal, find a taxi, and go to the bus station to catch a Greyhound to Long Beach. Problem solved.

Who was I kidding? I couldn't kill a teenager. Not with my shoulder. Also... I didn't actually like killing people. Even when they deserved it.

I went over and sat down next to the kid. I said, "You know, killing people isn't as much fun as it sounds."

"I never said it sounded fun."

"No. But you did make it sound like a rational response and it's not that either."

He shrugged. "That's your opinion."

"I've killed three men. In self-defense. Drowned one, stabbed one, shot one. I feel guilty. People think I shouldn't, but I can't help it. I think about those deaths and try to image scenarios where I didn't have to kill them, where I talked my way out of things, where it didn't come down to my life or theirs. They weren't good guys, they did bad things and they'd have kept doing bad things if I hadn't killed them. But the thing is, it's not up to me. I don't get to be judge and jury and executioner all rolled into one. And neither do you."

"You think you're a better person than I am."

"That's what you took from that?"

"You feel bad because you killed bad people. I think I'm going to feel bad if I don't."

There wasn't much I could say to that. I kept trying to come up with an argument that would convince him to go home and forget all this, but that didn't happen. After a while, the kid fell asleep.

I was going to have to figure out who killed Dom Reilly. I had no other choice. Now I really hoped The Partnership didn't kill him. I had experience with The Outfit in Chicago. A lot of experience. And I knew it was best if you kept those people as far away from you as possible.

We were going to have to talk to people who knew Dom and Joanne around the time of his disappearance. Maybe we shouldn't come right out and ask if there were any connections to The Partnership. Let people volunteer that information and then pretend to ignore it. What else? I was looking for motive. If I knew who might want him dead, then I had the possible murderer. Was he having an affair? Did he owe anyone money? Did he have enemies? Standard stuff, but it didn't hurt to remind myself.

The kid was still asleep when the United ticket counter opened at four-forty-five. A woman in her late twenties opened it up. She was pretty but not stewardess pretty. She wore a white, long-sleeved shirt with a burgundy tie. Over that was a navy sweater vest that had a United Airlines logo embroidered into it.

"Good morning, how can I help you?" she asked when I reached the counter.

"I'd like two tickets on your first flight to Detroit."

She clicked her CRT terminal a few times. Then a few more times. She looked up and smiled at me before she said, "It's a little slow first thing." A couple moments later she said, "Oh, there we go. Let's see... Yes, I have two tickets. Do you have a seat preference?"

"Aisle please."

The kid might want to sit by the window, but I was paying for these so screw him.

"All right then. I have a flight leaving at 5:15 with boarding beginning momentarily. That gets in to Denver at 8:37 mountain time. You'll have an hour and twenty-seven-minute layover. You'll leave at 10:04 and arrive in Detroit at 2:48 eastern time. You're lucky, you'll be getting breakfast *and* lunch."

Then she told me the price for two tickets, just over a thousand dollars, and I didn't feel so lucky. I handed her a credit card. She read my name off the card as she put it into the CRT. "Dominick Reilly. And your fellow passenger?"

"Cassidy Reilly."

She looked by me to Cass sleeping on the bench. "Son?"

"Nephew," I replied. Well, I certainly wasn't going to try and explain our actual relationship.

She ran my card through a credit card reader and made me sign the slip. As I did, she said, "I have you in seats 27D and 27E Reno to Denver and then seats 34B and 34C Denver to Detroit. The first flight isn't full so you should be able to spread out. The second flight is a little busier."

Then she printed out the tickets, took them out of the printer, folded everything up, and put it all into a custom folder about the size of an envelope.

"Your tickets are in here, your tickets serve as your boarding passes, no need to stop at the desk, you can get right on the plane. Your carbon is in there as well. Just go to gate C5. Any questions?"

"No, I think we're fine. Thanks."

I walked back to Cass and tapped his foot with mine. When he stirred, I said, "Come on, it's time to go." He followed me over to the security check like a zombie. I'd forgotten how deeply teenagers slept.

He put his backpack onto the conveyor belt and it went through the box. One after the other, we went through the walk-through scanner. I was second. Not surprisingly it went off just as it had at LAX.

"Stand over there on the X," he said.

As I did that, Cass went to pick up his backpack.

The guard said, "Hold on." Then went over and opened the backpack and rifled through it. I had no idea what was in there. I had a few nervous moments, but then I remembered the kid had gotten through LAX security just fine and he'd barely been out of my sight.

The security guy zipped the bag up. He was frowning, he'd probably have been happier if he'd found something. He reached under the conveyer and took out the metal-detecting wand. He came over to me and began waving it around me.

"I have screws and a plate in my shoulder blade."

He looked at me skeptically, found the spot with his wand, the reached out and poked around the spot with two fingers. That hurt like hell, but I kept quiet. I tried to blame all this on his being an old white guy trying to wield his tiny bit of power, but then I remembered we'd been there for hours, had a couple of intense conversations that might have looked like arguments, not to mention we barely had any luggage and weren't dressed for the weather—or at least I wasn't. We were probably lucky he wasn't strip-searching us. He finally let us pass and we went up an escalator to the gates.

When we reached the top, I said to Cass, "And that is why you don't buy a gun in Reno and try to bring it back to Detroit."

CHAPTER SIX

September 14, 1996
Saturday morning

The ticket agent was right. The flight was barely half full. The window seat next to us was empty. As soon as they closed the door, Cass moved over to that seat and promptly fell asleep as the stewardess explained how to buckle our seat belts. Then I drifted off for a bit myself.

I woke up in the middle of a scary dream about high-jackers going through the plane asking everyone to empty their pockets. So when the stewardess came by and asked if I wanted coffee, I said, "Absolutely," and lowered my tray.

Cass didn't wake up for coffee. I wondered if I should wake him and start asking him questions, but then we had almost six hours before we got to Detroit so it didn't matter much. Or at least I thought it was six hours. I wasn't sure how long we'd been in the air.

I sipped the thin, warmish coffee and thought about my life. A decision I'd made nearly ten years ago had come back to haunt me. Other decisions haunted me from that period but they were the ones I'd expected to haunt me. When I left Chicago the police really wanted to chat with me; I wondered if they still did. Detective Monroe White was probably retired.

Was there anyone left who remembered me? And if they did, did they care? Deanna Hansen remembered me. I was sure of that. In her mind, I owed her a lot of money and she wanted a pound of flesh for it. But maybe it didn't matter anymore. Her grandfather had left her in charge of his illegal enterprises, but she'd said she wanted to take the family business legit. Maybe she had. Claiming a debt without paper and threats of violence... that wasn't legit. So maybe she'd leave me alone. Not likely, but maybe. And then there was Rita Lundquist: crazy, psychotic and possibly not even alive. People in her line of crime don't always live long.

It was entirely possible that becoming Dom Reilly was the last decision that would ever haunt me. When I figured a way out of this, I might be done. I might be free and clear. That was a lovely thought.

The breakfast cart began making its way down the aisle. There weren't that many people so it would get to us fast. I woke Cass up. "Breakfast will be here in a minute. You should eat." He shifted in his seat then put his tray down.

Two of the stewardess' stopped the cart next to us. They were both young and pretty. One was barely older than Cass, with blond hair cut into a pixie. I glanced at him and noticed he was brushing his hair out of his eyes and watching her, intently but also shyly. The kid was obviously straight.

"Breakfast?"

"Yes, please."

We were each handed a plastic tray with a few bits of food on it. There were two coaster-sized pancakes, a single scrambled egg (not a combination I would have chosen), two desiccated sausages, a cup with bits of fruit and a four-ounce container of orange juice. The orange juice was the only item that tasted like real food.

I asked for more coffee. I wasn't going to let the fact that it wasn't very good stop me. I waited until we were both finished with our breakfasts before asking, "What do you remember about the time with your dad?"

"Not much."

"Do you know where you lived?"

"We lived in apartments. Clinton Township. Then my mom bought her house in Village Oaks."

"She bought the house after your father left?"

"Yeah. Couple years later I guess. I was seven, I think. I don't remember living in apartments very well. I mean, I know we did but I can't really remember."

I had no idea what kind of neighborhood Village Oaks was and wasn't sure I'd get a straight answer if I asked.

"You said your dad's mother and father are gone. What about siblings? Do you have aunts and uncles?"

"I have an Aunt Suzie. My father's sister."

"You see her much?"

"My mom doesn't like her. She's religious."

"And your mom. Her parents are still alive?"

He nodded.

"Does she have brothers or sisters?"

"She has two sisters. They don't talk to her much. She has an uncle she likes a lot."

The pretty blond stewardess came down the aisle with a plastic bag. She picked up our empty plastic breakfast trays. I watched Cass blush.

When she was gone, I asked, "You said you mom's at a casino in... Where was it?"

"Sault Sainte Marie. It's at the top of the mitten."

I kind of knew what that meant. "When will she be back?"

"Tomorrow night."

That meant we had tonight and all day tomorrow to ask around about her. That was good. I wanted to know as much as I could before I talked to her. *If* I talked to her. I still held out some hope that with a little more information I could get the kid to let go of the whole thing. I wasn't excited about meeting his mother. And why would I be? *Hello, I'm your fake husband* was not a sentence I ever wanted to utter. And not one she'd be happy to hear.

"Do you remember what your father did for a living?"

"Built cars. Plymouth Volare. My grandfather would point them out when I was a kid."

"So he made a good living?"

"I guess. I don't think they made those cars for long."

They didn't. Honestly I couldn't remember the last time I saw one. Did that mean he fell on hard times? There were lots of other places to build cars in Detroit, weren't there?

"Your mother likes to gamble. Did your dad?"

"I don't know. Maybe. I think they had card games in our apartment sometimes."

"When we were talking before, you mentioned a friend of your mother's. They were together when your parents met."

"Heather."

"Yeah. Are they still friends?"

"No. Not for a long time."

"Do you know her last name?"

He shrugged.

"You don't know how we can find her?"

"What difference does it make? You think she killed my dad?"

"We need to talk to people who knew your parents around the time your dad disappeared. They might know something."

"Why wouldn't they have said something before now?"

"They might not know they know anything. Or they think what they know doesn't mean anything. Don't you ever watch *Law & Order* or any of those shows?"

"I watch TV. I'm not stupid."

He was getting annoyed at me. I waited then tried again, and didn't do much better. "Your mom's family is Italian?"

"How do you know that?"

"Di Stefano is an Italian name, isn't it?"

"Nobody in our family is in the Mafia. Most Italian people aren't, you know."

"I know that."

To be fair, I was told his father was killed by The Partnership, an idea planted by his mother. We did need to find out if her family had any connection. And it didn't have to be a strong connection. Sometimes just knowing which coffee shop to go to was enough.

"Would anyone in her family know how to find someone in The Partnership?"

He didn't answer that. I could tell he didn't like the question. That ended our conversation for the moment. There were small TVs in the ceiling of the center aisle that popped down. They started showing an episode of *Seinfeld*. One of the stewardesses came around and asked if we wanted to rent headphones for three dollars. I passed. I wouldn't have taken one if they were free. I wasn't a fan of the show. The few times I'd seen it I thought the characters were too mean to each other to be funny.

I think I fell asleep for a while, because all of a sudden the show was over and the TVs were folding back into the ceiling. We needed to put up our trays and make sure our seat belts were on.

Then the plane began bouncing around. A few people kind of squeaked—not actual screams, the sound right before that. The one coherent thought I had while it was happening was that Ronnie would be really angry if I died in a plane crash without him. Not to mention, I'd told him I was in one city a few hours ago so dying in another city would be kind of annoying.

Things seemed to calm down and the captain came on the intercom. "Sorry about that folks. The wind in Denver is kind of famous. Nothing to worry about. We'll be on the ground in five minutes."

Ten minutes later we taxied into our gate. A bell tinged and the noises of the plan operating stopped. It didn't take us long to get off the plane. We walked passed the people waiting for friends and family; no one was there to meet us. We stopped and looked around.

This was a much bigger airport than Reno, but certainly not as big as LAX. I looked at our tickets and then the signage hanging above us. We were at gate B18 and we needed to go to B53. We had an hour and a half, so I figured we'd make it. I said as much to Cass and we started walking to our next gate.

In between the gates were different businesses, bars, snack bars. At a kind of intersection we found a newsstand. Since the kid was touchy, I decided I should really get some magazines for the next leg of our journey rather than question him anymore.

Madonna was on the cover of *Vogue*, which was about as much as I needed to know about that. *Time* had an article about the World Wide Web; okay, I'd read that. I flipped through *GQ* which had Elizabeth Shue on the cover in just a sweater. It seemed aggressively heterosexual for a magazine often referred to as *Generally Queer* and featuring an article by Gore Vidal. I decided I didn't really need to know all about the tweed coats for fall. *Us* had Julia Roberts on the cover, I took that. I looked through the paperbacks. At first I didn't want one, we only had two more hours in the air. But then, at some point I'd have to go home. I put a Sue Grafton book on my pile, *K Is for Killer*. I also grabbed a Denver Bronco's sweatshirt so I didn't freeze to death. It was orange. The only one in my size.

When I got up to the counter, Cass was purchasing four different kinds of candy. I wondered if it might keep him awake but then decided it wouldn't. And then, to add insult to injury, we stopped at a Mrs. Fields right before our gate. He got a chocolate chip cookie and I got two. I wasn't going to; we were getting lunch on the next flight. But then I remembered breakfast and had little hope for lunch.

A few minutes later, we arrived at our gate. We were one of the first. We sat down. Cass ate two Three Musketeer bars and I read *Us*. Eventually, I said, "So why don't you tell me about yourself. Just you and not your parents."

"What for?"

"So I can get to know you."

"Why do you want to get to know me?"

"Because I always like to be friendly with my kidnappers. It makes the whole experience more pleasant."

"You're not kidnapped."

"Oh? You mean I can go home and nothing bad will happen to me?"

"I didn't say that."

"Then I'm kidnapped."

"Whatever."

People started showing up. I could tell that this flight was going to be more crowded than the one from Reno. I got a couple of weird looks. Well, I was wearing an orange sweatshirt with a red turtleneck sticking out. Not to mention I was sitting next to a seventeen-year-old who radiated anger.

I flipped through my magazines for a while and then it was time to board. We were all the way at the back of the plane. Row 36. That meant we boarded last. Which, honestly, didn't make that much sense. You'd have thought we'd get to board first since we wouldn't have to struggle by anyone that way, but hey, I'm not in charge. When it was finally our turn, we made our way to the back of the plane. At our row, I saw that there was a woman in her forties sitting by the window. Her eyes were red and she held a pack of travel tissues in one hand. She was looking out the window, not as a way to see what was out there, but as a way to avoid our eyes.

For a moment, Cass looked like he might try to argue me out of the aisle seat but then gave up. He put his backpack under his seat and then flopped into it. I took my place on the aisle.

Once the plane took off and we reached altitude, I said to Cass, "Okay. If you won't tell me about yourself, why don't I tell you about you. You're mature for your age, too mature. You're smart but you only get B's. Your teachers always say you don't live up to your potential. You don't have a lot of friends. You like girls, but you're afraid of them. You don't know what you want to be when you grow up. You thought finding your dad would fix the things that are wrong with your life. Trust me, it wouldn't have."

He glowered for a few seconds before he said, "I'm not afraid of girls. Just the really pretty ones."

The woman next to the window had obviously heard most of that since she repositioned herself as though she were trying to get away from us. I decided to be a bit more careful. Or at least polite.

Our lunch was Salisbury steak and soggy fries. The sitcom they showed was *Mad About You*. I tried to read the mystery I'd bought but didn't get very far. I tried to stick to innocuous questions. I asked the kid, "Do you like living in Detroit?"

"I don't live in Detroit. I live in Novi. It's a suburb."

"Do you like school?"

"Who likes school?"

"I guess you're not thinking of going to college."

He frowned and said, "No. I'm not stupid."

"I don't think you're stupid. I also don't think going to college is stupid."

I didn't go to college, but that was mainly because if you grew up in Bridgeport in the sixties you didn't. I was busy trying to fit in, trying to be like everyone around me, so it didn't even occur to me that I *could* have gone. Some days I wonder who I might have been if I had gone to college. Hopefully not the kind of guy who was a magnet for trouble.

"Do you have a lot of friends?"

He turned and looked at me full on. "Do you wanna know my favorite color? It's green."

I didn't talk to him after that. Not until the plane landed. And even then, I didn't really say anything until we got out onto the concourse.

"When does your mother get home?"

"Tomorrow night."

I had the sinking feeling this would take a few days, so I said, "I'm going to need to rent a car and find a hotel."

He shook his head. "I have a car."

"That's great, but I still need to get from my hotel to wherever we're going."

He shook his head. "We have an extra bed in our junk room. You can stay in there."

"And when your mother comes home are you going to introduce me as your pet private detective?"

He shrugged and said, "No. I'm going to introduce you as Dominick Reilly. My father."

CHAPTER SEVEN

September 14, 1996
Saturday afternoon

The car had fins. A mint condition, two-door, tomato soup red 1958 Plymouth Belvedere sat on the second floor of the Big Blue Deck. The parking garage was directly across from the terminal we'd come from. As we got close to it, I asked, "This is your car?"

"Yeah."

"It's not really what I was expect—"

"My grandfather left it to me. He made it. I mean, not all of it. Some of it. He worked on the Plymouth line. My mother wanted to sell it, but Aunt Suzie wouldn't let her have the title. She pays the insurance for me."

His mother charges him room and board, but his aunt pays his car insurance. The kid was getting some very mixed signals—which could explain why he was desperate to have a father. He unlocked the door on the passenger side, and said, "Get in."

I climbed in. The seats were red-and-white vinyl that looked like they'd never been sat on. I glanced over at the driver's side and saw that the car had a push-button transmission. Cass climbed in and unlocked the anti-theft bar that held the steering wheel in position. He dropped the bar in the backseat.

I put on my safety belt. There was no shoulder strap, so if there was an accident I'd likely have significant whiplash. He put the key in the ignition and the engine burst into life. Pushing a gear, he pulled out of the parking spot and we were on our way.

We stopped at the cashier's booth and Cass paid the fee with a credit card. He'd given me the impression it was his mother's card, but I was starting to get the feeling that the name on the account wasn't related to either of them. A few minutes later we were heading west on one freeway, then quickly heading north on another. It was in the low fifties with dark clouds above us, and I had no idea where I was.

Not long afterward, we were in a neighborhood straight out of *Leave It to Beaver*. We pulled into the driveway of a two-story house with white painted brick on the first floor and matching clapboard on the second. The lawn was neat and the house surrounded with hydrangeas sending out last-gasp blossoms.

I followed Cass up to the front door. He got out a key and we walked in. We were in a small foyer with stairs on the far side and doors going into a living room, and opposite that a dining room. It was a more formal house than I'd been expecting.

"What do you want to do first?" Cass asked.

"Well, I'd like to take a shower."

The kid looked disappointed, so I said, "We're going need to talk to some people, I'd like a shower before we do that. You should probably take one, too. How many bathrooms do you have?"

"There's a half bath down off the kitchen and regular bathroom upstairs."

"So just one shower?"

"There's a bathroom with a shower off my mother's room, but we can't go in there."

Which meant it was exactly where I wanted to go.

"Do you want to shower first or do you want me to?"

"You can do it first. It's upstairs. The door's right there at the top of the stairs."

"Okay."

When I reached the top of the stairs, I noted one door to my right, two doors to my left and a door in front of me. I walked into the bathroom. It was large, with a bathtub and separate shower on the right side of the room, and a toilet and sink on the left. I guessed that the mother's room was the single door, and that her bathroom was on the other side of the wall from this bathtub and shower. I'd need to know that in a few minutes.

At first glance, the bathroom looked fairly ordinary: pink and gray with fuzzy rugs and seat covers. But then I looked closer. It was filthy. The toilet needed a good scrubbing, as did the sink, which was caked with toothpaste. I'd been thinking about rinsing out my shirt and boxer briefs but decided I'd be better off trying to stop and buy some new ones—plus I needed some kind of coat.

I opened the medicine cabinet—because that's who I am—and checked it out. There were some shaving supplies that went with the stray whiskers around the sink, a spray for jock itch, an unfinished prescription for antibiotics, allergy pills and a lot of Band-Aids.

The bright spot was the linen closet, which was largely empty but did hold one clean towel. I left the towel on the shelf, because I thought it might be the cleanest place in the bathroom, turned the shower on, and took off my clothes. When the water was warm enough I climbed in.

Did this disgusting bathroom mean anything? If they could afford a house like this, why didn't they have a cleaner? Or why didn't his mother clean the room? Sexist, I know, but most mothers would. Did she spend a lot of time screaming at him to clean up after himself and he just ignored her? Or did she not even bother?

Luckily, the water got hot. I turned around and let it run over the spot where I'd had surgery. The heat felt good. I'd taken all the aspirin; I needed to get more.

I should search the house. The comment he made about not going into his mother's room concerned me. If he wanted me to find his father's killer, he was going to have to do this my way. He didn't seem inclined to do that, though.

When I got out of the shower, I took the towel out of the linen closet and used it. Then I put my clothes back on. They didn't smell so great, but I'd hopefully make it to a store that afternoon. Then I opened the door as quietly as I could.

From downstairs, I heard music. Then a moment later talking. It took a moment, but I realized Cass was watching cable TV. MTV to be specific. Not that I knew much about it. We'd had cable at the house on

Second, but I didn't spend a lot of time watching MTV. Videos weren't my thing.

Creeping down the hallway, I opened each of the two doors. One was Cass's bedroom, which was messy and about as clean as the bathroom. There was a twin-sized bed, a dresser with a broken drawer and a desk. The desk was even more cluttered than the rest of the room. There was a pretty recent PC—I couldn't tell you much more than it looked new. And a laser printer; that I knew because we had one at The Freedom Agenda. On top of the printer was a Sony PlayStation. There was a stack of game cartridges piled next to the entangled electronics. The room smelled strongly of teenaged boy, so I decided not to stay long. I shut the door quietly.

The other room was what he'd described as the junk room. It seemed an accurate description. The room had an unmade twin bed pushed up against one wall, surrounded by stacks of boxes, folding chairs, bags filled with who knows what, an exercise bike, an abandoned Atari gameplayer and stacks of Harlequin romance novels. Since this was the room I was meant to stay in I didn't dig too deep, there would be time for that later.

I went back out to the top of the stairs and called down, "Your turn." I waited. A bit later the TV was turned off and Cass appeared at the bottom of the stairs. When he got closer, I said, "I peeked into the junk room. If you tell me where the sheets are, I'll make the bed."

"In the closet on the shelf," he said, as though that should have been obvious.

I went into the room and found them. I began making the bed, though mostly I was listening. I heard him go down to his room, then come back to the bathroom. A minute or so later, the shower came on. I left the junk room and quietly walked back to his mother's room. I opened the door.

It was a very large room with windows on opposite sides. There was her private bathroom and a walk-in closet. In the center of the far wall sat a very large four poster bed. It had a frilly canopy and looked like the kind of bed Scarlet O'Hara would enjoy. There was a floral love seat and a makeup table. The love seat had too many pillows and a comfy looking chenille blanket. The latest Harlequin romance was tangled in the blanket. The makeup table was covered with perfumes, tubes of lipstick, eyeshadow, mascara brushes, foundation, powder, eyelash curlers, tweezers, eyebrow pencils and thick brushes to spread it all around.

I took a look in her bathroom. It also had a lot of fuzzy pink rugs and things. These looked pretty new, and I had the feeling that as soon as they began to look shabby she'd put them into the other bathroom and buy new. Her towels looked recently purchased and there was a souvenir glass from Las Vegas holding her tooth brush next to the sink. I wouldn't say her bathroom was spotless, but it was definitely clean.

I opened the medicine cabinet. In addition to a selection of hairsprays, there was a row of prescription medications. I read the labels. The first bottle I picked up was Prozac. I'd heard of that. The bottle was full and the prescription was nearly a year old. She wasn't taking them. She was taking something called alprazolam. I wasn't sure what that was, but she was taking a lot of it. She'd only filled the prescription a month ago and it was nearly gone.

Back in the bedroom, I cracked the closet open. It was deep and crammed full. There was a lot of money in her bedroom. There was a lot of money in the house itself. Cass had mentioned that his mother had taken cards in her husband's name and never paid them. Just looking around the bedroom, I knew she was up to a lot more than that. Exactly what I couldn't be sure, but it did make me wonder how long she'd been up to it and whether it might have to do with Dom Reilly's disappearance.

Fortunately, the kid was taking a long shower. Longer than you'd expect from a kid with a high tolerance for filth. I went back into the junk room and finished making the bed. Then I went downstairs.

The living room was neat and expensively furnished. The only thing I could see that was out of place was Cass's backpack, which he'd left on one of the two facing sofas. There was a large mahogany coffee table with matching end tables. Against the walls were a couple of side chairs, a console television that looked like a liquor cabinet, and a cabinet that didn't but probably was. At the far end of the room was a double pocket door opening onto a den.

That room held a sturdy looking mahogany desk. There were a couple of short filing cabinets. I went in and sat behind the desk. There was a beige desk phone in one corner sitting on an answering machine, a stack of three yellow legal pads, a bunch of pens in a cup from the MGM Grand, and not much else. I opened the center drawer, and among the paperclips and receipts found an address book. It was old with a cartoon koala bear on the cover. I began flipping through it.

It was obvious she'd been using the book for a long time. It was probably time to replace it. First, I flipped to the R's. The first listing was for Patrick and Verna Reilly, but it was crossed out. Well, they were dead. Several names down was a listing for Suzie Reilly. Her address was crossed out and replaced by her parents', which was in Roseville. Wherever that was.

It didn't seem like something Joanne would forget, but I appreciated her letting me know Suzie had inherited her parents' home. I wondered if half the house had been left to her brother or whether her parents had given up and left it solely to her. I picked out a pen and wrote down her address and phone number. Not that I'd need it. I didn't think Cass would be letting me go anywhere on my own.

Then I flipped to D. There was an entire page of Di Stefanos. There was a Carmen and Ophelia Di Stefano. Ophelia was crossed off, so I assumed she'd died. My guess was these were Joanne's grandparents. I had no idea which of these Di Stefanos I should talk to. Cass would have to tell me.

Though the book was pretty full, I realized the oldest addresses were at the top of the page. I flipped through the alphabet looking for one in particular. I didn't find it until I got to the letter S. Szymanski. Heather Szymanski. My guess was that this was the Heather who'd been with Joanne when she met Dom Reilly. I quickly scanned through the S's to see if she had another listing. It made sense that she might have moved. There wasn't one.

Well, she could have gotten married and changed her name. That meant she could be under any letter. I opened both bottom drawers looking for a telephone book. It was on the right. The drawer on the left was locked. I decided to deal with that in a bit. I grabbed the phonebook.

I got lucky. Heather Szymanski was listed. I wrote her name and address down on the pad. Then I put the phonebook back so I could tackle the locked drawer. First, I pulled out the drawer above it. As I'd expected, there was a thin piece of unfinished veneer between the drawers. At some point, someone had tried to break through it, so I could see into the drawer below. There was an accordion folder in there. The hole wasn't large enough for me to get my fingers through, so I had no idea what was in there. I felt the bottom of the drawer above, then put it back. Then I felt the bottom of all the other drawers. Taping a key to the bottom of a drawer was an easy way to hide it. Just not this time.

The smart thing would be to keep the key on your key ring or, at the very least, hidden in a different room. Most people didn't do the smart thing. I found Joanne's key when I took all the pens out of the MGM Grand cup and flipped the cup over. The key fell out.

After I opened the drawer, I took out the accordion folder and looked it over. In the first pocket were about ten letters sent to different individuals explaining that their debt had been purchased and was now owed to Top Dawg Collections. That matched the name at the top of the stationery. Each letter was signed by Cassidy Reilly, administrative assistant.

It seemed all wrong. Was Top Dawg Collections where Joanne worked? Cass had just said she worked for a lawyer who did collections. Lawyers usually worked under their names.

The file made it seem like Joanne had her own collection business. Each letter had notes that reflected how many phone calls had been made to the debtor. A lot of them. Enough to qualify as harassment.

The next pocket contained bank statements for Top Dawg Collections. The account had well over fifty thousand dollars in it. Fifty two thousand six hundred and eighty-five to be exact. That was a lot of money.

The next pocket held a packet of papers which were the LLC Operating Agreement for Top Dawg Collections. I flipped through it. It was pretty simple with the members being Cassidy Reilly and L&J Holdings, LLC. There were several empty pockets, and then in the last there was a number 10 envelope. I opened it and found six credit cards. Two of the names on the cards matched letters in the first pocket.

It took me a moment to work that out. People with debts in collection were often in a lot of financial trouble, but not all. Sometimes it's a forgotten hospital bill or a credit card company that lost track of you. Those people might still be able to get new credit, albeit at higher rates. She was taking out cards—

Something hit me. When Cass said he'd taken one of his mother's credit cards, he hadn't meant one of *hers*. He'd meant one of the ones she kept in this envelope. They were hers but not hers. They were definitely not cards she'd be paying for. Suddenly, I was annoyed with the kid. He'd let me pay for very expensive plane tickets from LAX to Reno and Reno to Detroit. Granted, I wouldn't have accepted, but he didn't even offer.

Upstairs, the shower finally stopped. I put everything back into the desk, ripped off the page I'd been writing on, and walked out of the office. I wanted to look at the rest of the house before Cass got dressed and came downstairs. I went the living room, crossed the foyer, and was in the dining room. There was a lovely dining table with six chairs, thick drapes, a China closet with a few pieces sitting in it, a soup tureen shaped like a rabbit and a mixing bowl. I walked through to the kitchen. It was a nicely designed room with newish appliances. The first thing I did was open the refrigerator. It was full; and yet it wasn't.

There was an entire shelf of Diet Coke in cans. The top shelf was packed with leftover take-out in white boxes. The vegetable bin was filled with packets of catsup, mustard, mayonnaise and soy sauce. There were two bottles of champagne. I opened the freezer compartment and found a frozen pizza and a half-eaten container of vanilla ice cream. It seemed pretty scant for a woman who was charging her seventeen-year-old son board.

I opened some of the cupboards, which were mostly empty. She was definitely committed to this no-cooking thing. She didn't even have anything to do it with. I pulled open the drawers. One held silverware, one held take-out menus from dozens of restaurants and the rest were empty.

The kitchen had a built-in breakfast nook and a sliding door out to the patio. There was a door that I thought might lead to the garage. It did.

Inside the two-car garage sat a recent model, bronze Cadillac Eldorado. There was more in the garage than there was in her kitchen cupboards but not by much. I didn't see a lawn mower so she must hire a company to do that. Most people would pay their teenage son to mow the lawn. But, given the state of his room, I could see why she might not.

"What are you doing out here?" Cass asked, standing in the door to the kitchen. His hair was wet so he was obviously clean, but it looked like he'd put the same clothes back on. I was already getting tired of the red hoodie.

"Snooping. That's how we're going to figure out who killed your father. By snooping."

"Yeah, well, my mother's car didn't kill him."

"She likes expensive things, doesn't she?"

"Do people like being poor?"

"How far is she willing to go to have money?"

"What does that mean?"

I decided not to tell him I'd been rifling through her desk and knew about her (or their) cagey little games with credit cards.

"You told me she took out credit cards in your dad's name after he disappeared. You don't think that was a little dishonest?"

"She was a single mom. He abandoned her."

"She seems to have done all right."

"I know she bends the rules. That doesn't mean she killed my dad."

Seemed like a good idea to drop it. "I'd like to go see your aunt."

"Which one?"

"Your father's sister. Suzie."

"Sure, I'll call her."

"Let's just go."

"How come?"

"Because she might say sure, come by on Tuesday. I want to see her today. I don't want to be here very long."

"Yeah, okay. Come on."

CHAPTER EIGHT

September 14, 1996
Saturday late afternoon

The house was on Dugan Street in Roseville. It was one of those split-level houses that was popular in the late sixties and early seventies. The bottom half was part basement. The front door and tiny foyer floated between the two floors with a short stairway running up or down to either floor.

We climbed out of the Belvedere and walked up the cement walkway to the front door. It was election season and the lawn was decorated with political signs: CLINTON/GORE, LEVIN FOR SENATE, BONIOR, NO ON E. After Clinton, none of that made much sense to me.

After we rang the bell it took a minute or two for Suzie Reilly to answer. She was a thickset woman wearing a pair of jeans and men's cotton work shirt. Her hair was graying and cropped short, and her skin was nearly as white as snow. My gaydar went into four alarm mode.

"Hey," Cass said. "Can we come in and talk to you?"

"Of course, you can. I'll make some coffee real quick. Make yourselves comfortable in the dining room."

Before she walked up the short flight of stairs to the main floor, she gave me a suspicious glance. As she should. I followed Cass into the house.

On the main floor, the living room was one of those sets you buy from the back of the newspaper for a scandalously low, low price. Four or five or six matching pieces. Sofa, love seat, not-so-comfortable chair in a thick, scratchy brown fabric. Coffee table and end tables. There was a reproduction of the Last Supper on the wall above the sofa.

The dining area was off the living room. It was pretty bare, other than the table and chairs and a large crucifix on the wall. I was sensing a theme. Cass made himself comfortable at the far end of the table. I sat at the other end, far less comfortably. I could hear a Mr. Coffee chugging away in the kitchen, when Suzie came through the swinging door and set a bowl of sugar and a creamer on the table.

"All I have is skim. Cutting down on fat. I hope that's okay," Then she went in for the kill, "And you are?"

That was a tough question. Cass tried to field it starting out, "He's, uh..."

Avoiding the idea of a name completely, I said, "I work with a charity. Loosely affiliated with Big Brothers of America. We help unite kids with their parents. Cass wants to find his father."

I was very proud of the fact that one of those sentences was true. Cass did want to find his father. Suzie looked at me skeptically but then turned to study Cass.

"You want to find your father? Why didn't you ever say anything? You always act like you're perfectly fine with just Joanne."

"I don't know. It just... It seemed like a good idea."

"Do you need money? Are you in trouble? Is Joanne not taking care of you?"

"I'm seventeen. She doesn't need to take care of me. I just want to find my dad. Can you talk to... this guy?"

"If you want me to, of course. Let me get cups."

I stared at Cass for a moment. I wanted to say, "Fuck, why didn't we think of a cover story on the way over." Well, I knew why. The kid was difficult and I barely wanted to talk to him most of the time. Sure, I felt bad for him. But I also didn't trust him. That was not a good combination.

Aunt Suzie was back. She had the pot of coffee and three mugs hanging from the fingers of one hand. She'd clearly been a waitress at one time. Normal people don't carry mugs like that. She plunked the mugs onto the table and poured us each a cup of coffee. Then she sat down at the table.

Aunt Suzie and I took our coffee black. Cass loaded up on milk and sugar.

"All right. Go ahead."

"Your brother disappeared in 1982?"

"Yeah. July. Around the twenty-first. We're not really sure. Joanne claims she came home on the twenty-first and all his things were gone. No one has seen or heard from him since."

"And the last time anyone saw him? Other than Joanne."

"Probably a few days before the twenty-first."

"But you would have been there," I said to Cass.

"I was four."

"Yes, I remember that. But you might have been there."

"And he might not have been there," Suzie said. "He could have been with Joanne's mother or someone in her family or even a friend." To Cass she said, "You were passed around a lot. I'm sorry, but it's true."

"So you think he wasn't there the night Dom left?"

"No, I don't think so."

"Tell me about your brother, just in general."

"Dominick was good-looking, really good-looking. But I don't think he knew it. He talked about Joanne like he didn't deserve a girl as pretty as she was. But I think he could have done better. He just didn't know it."

I took a sip of my coffee and waited, hoping she'd go on. "He wasn't book smart, but he had common sense. He certainly wasn't street smart. We come from decent hard-working people and that's all he wanted to be. He loved building cars. He loved everything about them."

"What can you tell us about his marriage?"

"It gave us Cass." She turned and smiled at him. "That's the only good thing I can say about it."

"I know Cass is sitting right here, but I need you to be as honest as you can be."

She looked over at the boy and he nodded, giving her permission.

I asked, "Do you know specifically what was wrong with their marriage."

"Well, Joanne was what was wrong. She's a bitch. And I don't call other women names lightly." She paused and sipped her coffee. "Nothing was ever good enough for her. And Dominick gave her everything he could, but she was never happy. It was never enough."

"Do you know what might have been happening right before he disappeared?"

She sighed. "They were fighting a lot, more than usual. Joanne wanted to go back to school to be a paralegal."

"And he said no?"

She shook her head. "He said yes. But he wanted her to wait until Cass was in school all day. It would have been two years. I thought he was being reasonable. Everyone thought he was being reasonable."

"So he disappeared and she became a paralegal?"

"She signed up for some course almost right away. My parents would babysit for her. Not because they wanted to help her, but it was really the only way to see Cass. It wasn't a long class, and then she was working for Mr. Cray in Novi. Almost right away."

"And this is the guy she still works for?"

"Yeah," Cass said.

I decided to ask about him later, when Cass and I were alone. I changed direction. "Did your parents ever report your brother missing?"

"Of course they did. Nothing happened, though."

"Do you know why?"

"Because the police believed Joanne. She said he ran off and they believed her."

"All his things were gone," Cass said.

"She could have packed them up and gotten rid of them," Aunt Suzie said. Her voice was gentle and kind. I got the impression she'd been waiting a long time for this conversation. She was probably right, too, since we proved she'd sold his papers. I glanced at the kid. There was struggle on his face. He seemed unprepared for the direction this might take.

"He must have had a car," I said.

That brought a smile to her face. "Boy did he have a car. A '68 Plymouth Barracuda. Fastback. Matador red. Lord, he loved that car. Babied it. Washed it every week. It was in amazing condition."

"So that's a family thing? You Reillys love your Plymouths?"

"I've got a Voyager in the garage."

Not on par with a classic from the fifties or sixties, but I smiled anyway. "If your brother didn't run off, what do you think happened to the car? Chop shop?"

She shrugged. "In 1982 there would have been a number of possibilities. Chop shop, yes. Or it could have been smuggled out of the country and sold somewhere that doesn't look too closely at registrations. If you wanted to keep it in the US—well, by that point there would have been a lot of Barracudas in junkyards, so you could have swapped a couple of VINs with a car that's been totaled."

"Wait. Explain that a little more. I know what a VIN is, but why do you need more than one?"

"Ah. The VIN number for each car is put in various locations. That car had the number on the dashboard. The same number would have been somewhere in the engine. And also on the frame. Some of the locations are easy to change out, others are not. You change the number in a couple of locations and then get a salvage title based on the totaled vehicle. It would have lowered the value of the car, but that doesn't always matter. Plus, there are ways to get a clean title at some point."

"So the car just disappeared?"

"Maybe. As far as I know it's never been found—not that the police are looking for it. It wouldn't have been hard to drive it down to Indiana or Ohio and do a private sale. It could be legally registered and insured somewhere and we'd have no idea. Particularly if it's on its third or fourth owner."

"Do you have the VIN number?"

"I don't. I wouldn't. It would be with Dom's things. Which Joanne says are long gone. Maybe it's somewhere in her house, but she's not about to let us search for it."

She glanced at Cass, but he was looking at the ceiling. I tried to figure out if she'd ever asked to be allowed to search the house. She might not have. Clearly, he was touchy about his mother. Backing off, I said, "Even if we found the car, it wouldn't mean anything. Dom could have sold it himself."

I decided not to mention that if Dom was at the bottom of Lake Erie his car might be with him. Not to mention there were about a thousand other lakes in Michigan he could be at the bottom of.

"Did your brother have any connection to The Partnership?"

"Was he in the mob? No. He wasn't."

"I meant, would they want to get rid of him for any reason?"

"Not that I'm aware of. He'd been in and out of work for a while. The Plymouth plant he was working at closed and got sold to GM. But they were going to take most of the guys on so things were looking up."

"How were they getting by?"

"Unemployment, odd jobs he'd pick up. They were okay. I mean, it wasn't enough for Joanne, but nothing's enough for Joanne."

"What about friends? Anyone you think we should talk to?"

"I still see Dick Potter every so often. If I go back to the old neighborhood."

"The old neighborhood?"

"We grew up in Corktown. My parents bought this house in 1972. I was just out of high school. I don't think Dick knows anything. I mean, he and I have talked about this for years."

I asked for his phone number but avoided saying the obvious. If this guy did know something unflattering about Dom he probably wouldn't tell his sister. And it was almost always unflattering things that led to murder.

"You believe your brother's dead, don't you?"

"I know he's dead. He wouldn't have broken off contact with my parents. Never."

"And he's never been declared dead by a court?"

"Joanne wouldn't do it, and as his wife it's really up to her. She claims he's alive, but she's a liar. Sorry, Cass, but she is. When my parents passed away they left this house to me and Dominick. He owns half of it. Of course, Joanne has asked for his half in cash. Says she's owed it for child support."

"Wouldn't it be hers if she had him declared dead?"

"No. The way the will is written it goes to Cass if Dominick is gone."

"What did you tell her when she asked for money?"

"This was five, six years ago. I offered to take Cass off her hands if she was having trouble taking care of him." To Cass she said, "I'd invite you to stay for dinner, but it's my league night and I'm meeting a couple of friends at Coney Island."

I assumed Coney Island was some kind of restaurant, she obviously wasn't flying to New York City for dinner. She'd be pretty hungry before she got there.

Cass hugged his aunt goodbye at the door. There was an awkward moment where she could have said, "It was nice to meet you..." But I hadn't ever said my name. The look on her face said she was very aware of that.

Once we were in the Belvedere, Cass asked, "Where to now?"

"I'd like to stop somewhere and buy a jacket and maybe some under-wear. And some dinner might be nice."

Ten minutes later, Cass had found a K-Mart. Like most department stores they were ahead of the weather. The coats were mainly winter jackets. More than I needed. I picked out a navy blue crew neck sweater and a black puffer vest to go over it. I grabbed a pack of boxer briefs and some white socks. On the way out I snagged a large bottle of Tylenol.

"Why are you taking so much aspirin and shit?"

"I got shot. Christmas of eighty-four. In one side, out the other. The bullet went through my right shoulder blade. They screwed it all back together temporarily. I was supposed to get it all done again, but life got in the way. Last month I took a fall and it all came apart. They went in and screwed it all together again. Still hurts."

Saying it all made me feel a bit like Humpty Dumpty.

"Who shot you?"

"I ruined a woman's plan to get rich. She'd probably shoot me again if she knew where I was."

I decided to leave out the part where the fall I took was because I'd ruined a woman's plan to get away with murder. Ruining women's plans... There's something there I might want to think through.

The cashier rang me up quickly and I paid with my credit card. The total was nearly a hundred dollars. Most of it was the puffer vest. On the way back to the car, I said, "Tell me about Mr. Cray."

"He's my mom's boss."

"And..."

"He's old. Married. He's got like six kids."

"What is old to you? Your mom's age or your grandparents' age?"

"Like in the middle."

"So, fifty?"

"Yeah, I guess."

That was sobering. I'd be fifty in two years. And yes, when I was seventeen I would have thought that was old. It just didn't seem as old as it used to.

It was easy to find the car since it was almost four decades older than everything else there. He unlocked his door and got in. I waited for him to reach over and unlock the passenger door. When he did, I put my bag on the floor and climbed in.

"What else? Do they get along?"

"She thinks he's great. Most of the time." He was taking the anti-theft bar off the steering wheel.

"And when she doesn't think he's great?"

"She just likes to get her way. Everyone does, don't they?"

"She's worked for him a long time, right?"

He turned the key and pushed the R button. "Yeah, I guess twelve years or so."

"Your mom went to work for him right after she became a paralegal?"

"Yes."

"Do you know how she paid for her schooling?"

He shrugged. As we drove out of the parking lot, I asked, "How'd your mom find the job?"

"I don't know."

"She never said?"

"I guess she got it the normal way. Like through a newspaper ad or something. These aren't important questions. My mom's job doesn't have anything to do with what happened to my dad."

"So what does?"

He didn't say anything. We sat at a red light. I asked, "Do you think Mr. Cray might have connections with The Partnership?"

"He's a lawyer."

"They have lawyers, believe me. Haven't you ever seen *The Godfather*?"

"We're Italian. We boycott movies like that. They're all made up."

CHAPTER NINE

September 14, 1996
Saturday, early evening

We ate Taco Bell in the car. I would have thought he'd be more careful of the car. It really was in beautiful condition, but I was getting the feeling in a year it would look a lot like his bedroom.

When I finished my grilled, stuffed chicken burrito, which I barely considered food, I said, "You mentioned your mother's friend, Heather. They were together when your mom and dad met. I'd like to see her next."

"I don't know where she lives. She was never really around."

"I found her in the phone book."

"I don't know her last name, so how do—"

"I looked in your mother's address book. The one with a koala bear on the cover."

"You went in my mother's desk? She's going to be so pissed."

"You went in your mother's desk. You stole one of her illegally obtained credit cards. She'll figure that out eventually."

"She said I could use one in an emergency."

I didn't believe him, so I asked, "And what emergency are you experiencing? Exactly?"

He clamped his mouth shut as his face turned red. Then drove us to the Corktown neighborhood in downtown Detroit where Heather Szymanski lived. It was a silent half an hour and we passed through a number of neighborhoods featuring hundreds of political signs. Clinton seemed to be winning over Dole, while most of the other signs continued to confuse me. The names seemed to change a lot, probably local stuff I didn't know anything about.

"What's E?" I asked Cass.

"They want to have casinos in Detroit. My mom's all excited."

We drove down Rosa Parks Boulevard and turned onto Marantette Street. The house Heather lived in was two-stories and had once been a single family house. It was now divided into apartments. An extra door had been added on the first floor next to the original front door making it all look chopped up.

After we parked the car and Cass put his anti-theft bar onto the steering wheel, we walked up to the house. He looked around suspiciously —I think he was concerned about the neighborhood but he didn't say anything.

The neighborhood didn't look great. Which didn't mean anything one way or another. I knew of a lot of neighborhoods in Los Angeles that looked fine even when they weren't. What I *did* recognize was the fear of a suburbanite visiting the big city in Cass's eyes.

I rang the doorbell, which we could hear quite well on the stoop. Seconds later, footsteps came down the stairs. Locks were opened. Three. Then finally, the door.

Standing there was a woman in her mid-thirties. She had long straight sandy hair, light blue eyes, and freckles on her cheeks. She wore a peasant dress that was years out of style and splashed with paint here and there. She looked from me to Cass, and then said, "Oh my God, Cass... is that you?"

He nodded.

"You look just like your dad." Recognizing that was a sore subject, she mumbled the word, "Shit." Then she looked at me and back at Cass.

"This is a friend of mine," he said.

She looked worried. I decided to drop the Big Brother lie. I wasn't convinced it worked. I said, "I'm kind of a private investigator. Cass wants to find his father. I understand you're a friend of his mother, Joanne Reilly."

"I was. But that was a long time ago. Cass, how can you afford a private investigator?"

Before he could stutter and stumble his way through that, I said, "There was a bit of money when his grandparents died. He just came into it."

"Why don't you come up stairs," she said, stepping aside so we could get to the stairs. Once we were both past her, she shut and relocked the door. We went up the stairs, which were wooden and showed the effects of having been trod upon for about a century.

At the top of the stairs was another door, also with a lock. We walked through it, but Heather didn't lock it behind us. We were standing in a kitchen that hadn't been updated in decades. The appliances didn't match. The stove was white and shaped like a Buick from the fifties, while the refrigerator was harvest gold. In the center of the room was a table and chairs.

On the right, there was a closed door which must have led to the bedroom and bathroom. To the left, pocket doors opened onto a large living room that took up half the floor. It was immediately obvious why she lived here. The room had been turned into an art studio. There were a couple of easels, one large, one small. Both had half-finished paintings on them. There was a table with brushes, glasses filled with mucky water, tubes of paint and dribbled paint all over it. A tarp had been put beneath the table and it, too, was covered in dribblings. There were finished paintings stacked against the walls, and several hung on the walls.

Heather's style was colorful and abstract, flirting with geometric but never fully committing. It probably didn't belong in a museum but looked like it might be at home above a sofa. Speaking of sofas, she had one shoved up against the large uncovered windows at one end of the room.

"I really have no idea what happened to Dom," she said, without offering us anything to drink or even a seat.

"I'm hoping you can tell us about Dom and Joanne when you knew them. I understand you were with Joanne when they met?"

"I was. Joanne and I were pretty wild as teenagers. We loved disco music. I remember skipping school with her and going to a movie theater and watching *Saturday Night Fever* over and over again. We were younger when that came out though. By the time we met Dom, it was all about Donna Summer, I think. We loved her. 'Last Dance'. We started going out a lot that year. To clubs and places. Joanne had gotten us fake IDs. In the daylight they were obvious fakes but at night... well, now I think they let us in *because* we were so young. We always had great clothes, great makeup, shoes that made us six feet tall. Joanne taught me how to shoplift so it was... Sorry Cass, I don't mean to make your mother sound awful."

"Stores charge too much," he said with a shrug. "They factor it in."

"That doesn't mean—"

"Was it always just the two of you?" I asked.

"Oh, no. Joanne knew how to make friends. We knew people everywhere we went. Boys mainly. Men, I guess I'd consider them now."

"Do you remember any names?"

"Oh gosh. Well, Joanne's cousin Luca Amato was around a lot. Hector Verde, of course. Allen something. He was sweet. He would always dance with me while Joanne danced with other guys. And Dom... of course."

"So she met Dom and they became boyfriend and girlfriend?" I filled in.

She hesitated before saying, "Basically. It never seemed that serious between them, but then they got married."

"And you stayed friends after the marriage? You gave her a baby shower?"

"At first it was all very exciting. Joanne had an apartment and a husband and a baby. It was very grown up. But then, well, apartments need to be cleaned, husbands fed, and babies... well, they need everything. I know her sisters helped a lot, and Dom's sister, Suzie. Their parents, too. I even babysat a few times so they could go out dancing. But then I went to college and I didn't have much time... and we grew apart."

"You weren't around much when Dom disappeared?"

"That was a strange time. Everyone knew about it and... well, it was like he died except there was no wake, no funeral, nothing. I went see Joanne once and she wasn't very friendly. She criticized me for not being around, even though I was in college and did return her calls whenever... Anyway. I knew it was a bad time so I just let her say whatever. I tried calling a few weeks later. She just let her answering machine pick up. And then she never called back."

"So you don't know much about what was going on right before Dom disappeared," I said.

"Not firsthand no. But…" She glanced at Cass before she went on. "I heard things. Everyone heard things."

"What things?" I asked.

"I'm not sure I want to say."

"You need to."

"It can't get back to Joanne. I don't think she'd like our talking about this."

I looked at Cass. Eventually, he said, "I won't say anything. Promise."

Joanne took a moment. And why wouldn't she? Seventeen year-olds were hardly the most trustworthy people in the world.

"I don't know anything. Not for certain. There's always been a rumor that Joanne had Luca kill Dom. You could have heard that anywhere."

"Her cousin, Luca?"

She looked at Cass again. The boy didn't look happy.

"It's a rumor," she said.

"Is Luca in The Partnership?"

"That's another rumor. Rumors aren't always true. I mean, you just have to be Italian and people say you're in the mob."

That was true, not to mention Italians didn't have a monopoly on organized crime.

"Do you know Luca well?" I asked Cass.

He nods. "My mom loves him."

Heather was silent. Uncomfortably so. I asked her, "Do you believe Luca killed Dom?"

"I think he would have done anything Joanne asked. And, yes, I think she might have asked."

I waited a bit, just to let that sink in for Cass. Then I said, "Well, we'll get out of your way. Thank you. You've been helpful."

The three of us clomped down the stairs, said goodbye—well, Heather and I said good-bye. Cass was growing more sullen by the moment—and then she locked the door up again. As we walked to the car, which was miraculously still there. I asked, "Do you want me to drive?"

He ignored me and got into the driver's seat. I'd barely shut the door when he pulled away from the curb. I couldn't believe he'd gotten the anti-theft bar off so fast.

"She's a lying bitch."

I assumed he meant Heather, though I suspected it was more true about his mother. I asked, "Which part were lies?"

"All of it."

"Your mother doesn't have a cousin named Luca?"

"He owns a trucking company. He's not in The Partnership."

Setting aside the stereotypical idea of a mobster owning a trucking company as a cover, I said, "Heather didn't say he was in The Partnership. She said other people thought that. She was actually pretty nice about it."

"My mom didn't ask anybody to kill my dad, okay?"

"Okay, sure."

We were back on a freeway pretty quickly. I really had no idea where we were. I was feeling pretty uncomfortable about that, and that I was in the company of a very angry teenager who couldn't be rational when it came to his mother.

"Look, when you do this kind of investigation you have understand that you're not necessarily going to find out things you want to know."

"I know my mother didn't have anything to do with it."

See, not very rational.

"We know whoever killed your dad is violent and smart. So maybe we should stop. I'm not sure it's safe to get too close to someone who'd do this. We could be putting ourselves in danger. We could be putting your mom in danger."

He didn't say anything. After a couple of minutes, I turned the dial on the radio. AM only. It must have been near the top of the hour since the news was on. Bob Dole was visiting Michigan. Someplace called Midland, which was presumably in the center of the state. They were planning to re-introduce the two-dollar bill. That didn't seem like a great idea. They'd tried it around the bicentennial and nobody was much interested.

Cass reached over and turned the radio off. After a moment, he said, "Maybe it was Luca. But that doesn't mean my mom had anything to do with it. Maybe he did it as a favor without her asking."

"And she's been covering it up for a decade? Doesn't that make her just as guilty?"

"No. Not *as* guilty. Not really guilty at all."

We parked in front of the house. I got the impression he wasn't allowed to park in the driveway. He put the anti-theft bar onto the steering wheel and got out. I followed him up the lawn to the front door. After he unlocked it we went inside.

Cass walked directly over to the cabinet and opened it. I hadn't realized that it was a liquor cabinet, fully stocked. He poured a highball glass full of something red and sticky. It looked like raspberry liquor—not Chambord, which came in a distinctive bottle, but some cheap knockoff.

He saw me looking at him, and asked, "You want some?"

"No thanks. I'm going to bed."

It was barely eight-thirty.

CHAPTER TEN

I suppose I could have had a drink with him. As I've said, I didn't drink because it loosened my tongue. Cass knew my secrets though so it might not have been a big deal. On the other hand, the boy was a danger to me. Drinking with him would have been foolish.

Upstairs in the junk room, I did not go to sleep. I wouldn't have even if that had been my plan. Cass was playing music. CDs? Possibly record albums? Either way, the volume was cranked up. I wasn't sure if there was a turntable or a CD player in one of the cabinets in the living room or I'd simply not noticed it in the office. His taste—or more likely Joanne's—ran to early eighties new wave: The Police, The Go-Go's, Talking Heads. It was taking me back.

I tried not to think about my misspent youth since I was clearly misspending my middle age. Instead, I opened boxes. Quickly, I realized it was called the junk room because it really was full of junk. A lot of the boxes held things from Cass's childhood. They seemed to move backward through time, the most accessible boxes more recent. One seemed to be from Cass's fourteenth year: A *Jurassic Park* T-Shirt, a frayed pair of carpenter jeans, several hoodies. There was a Gameboy and six cartridges.

Another held his clothes from aged twelve. He'd been small for his age—he was still small for his age. There were a couple of books that seemed to skew younger. The only way I was sure he was twelve at this point was that there was a stack of comics from 1991. I checked the copyright pages.

Some of the boxes were obviously Joanne's, like the one that had three Jane Fonda VHS tapes and a half dozen Lycra exercise outfits in bold purples and pinks. There were also several boxes of financials, including Joanne's taxes from 1992 and 1993. Both looked as though they were filed late, so I guessed that 1994 and 1995 hadn't been filed yet.

I scanned through, attempting to glean what I could. Her salary for each of the two years was $44,000. Not bad, but also not enough to support the way she was living. I continued to scan through. The only other interesting thing on the forms was that her mortgage interest deduction was nearly eleven thousand dollars. I had no idea how much houses in Detroit area were worth, but it did seem like a lot of interest.

I dug around some more and found her bank statements. She banked with Fifth Third. These were from '94 and the whole year was there. There wasn't a lot of information. Transactions were identified by check number and date, and not much else. I was able to see that she received an automatic deposit every two weeks for $1,362.

Okay, there was something interesting. Every month she sent out a check for $2,232. That had to be her mortgage payment. That left roughly four hundred dollars a month to live on. But she didn't have to worry too much. The balance in her checking account never seemed to dip below eleven thousand dollars.

I scanned through for additional deposits. Randomly, there were deposits for a few hundred dollars here and there, up to five hundred. They happened several times a month. I also noted that, aside from writing checks, she never took any cash out of the account. There didn't seem to be any ATM withdrawals. Did that mean she was walking around with absolutely no cash in her pocket? Somehow I doubted that.

I dug deeper into the box and found two more bank accounts: One at 1st State Bank and another at Community Bank. Both of these accounts were in the name of Joanne Reilly, though it seemed she usually used her maiden name. I gathered the statements from April '94 and was able to trace money moving from 1st State to Community, and then finally to

Joanne Di Stefano's account at Fifth Third. The deposits to these additional accounts were several thousand dollars and monthly.

The statements told me a few things. They each had a deposit once a month, which was always more than Joanne took out of the accounts. Also, I suspected these accounts had something to do with Top Dawg Collections downstairs. I had the feeling she was up to something illegal. I just wasn't sure what exactly.

I opened the closet and began looking around. I found what was probably the earliest of Cass's boxes. It was full of his baby clothes, including a pair of impossibly small, stonewashed jeans, a Detroit Lions onesie and a baby-sized Hawaiian shirt. Underneath the clothing I found a baby book. When I opened it, an invitation to Cass's baby shower fell out with a carefully printed list of those who attended. The shower wasn't part of the book. I quickly determined that Heather was the one to give her the shower since the invitation was homemade: a cute sketch of a duck, which was then copied onto yellow copy paper. The list of guests was artfully printed onto a similar piece of paper. I set the list aside and flipped the pages of the book. They were all empty. Joanne hadn't made a single entry in the baby book. Obviously, she wasn't sentimental. But then why did she still have Cass's baby clothes?

At the very end of the book, a Catholic baptismal certificate had been stuck there. At the top of the page it listed the church as St. Margaret of Scotland. Then it had Cass's name, Cassidy Matteo Reilly. His parents' names. That he was born at St. John Hospital. The officiating priest was named Di Stefano—likely a relative of Joanne's. Heather Szymanski and Luca Amato were named as sponsors.

I returned to the list of women who were at Joanne's baby shower. Heather, of course. Suzie Reilly. Josette and Angelina Di Stefano. Verna Reilly—Dom's mother, Carla and Rose Amato—who were probably cousins of Joanne's, and Mama Di Stefano.

Would it be worth talking to any of them? Dom's mother was gone so that wasn't possible. And we'd already talked to Suzie. I definitely wanted to talk to Joanne's sisters, preferably before she came back on Sunday night. One of the cousins might be a good idea... Wait. There was only one friend on the list. Heather. Why weren't there more? Well, I suppose a seventeen-year-old wife and mother might not have a lot in common with her classmates. And... I was getting the impression Joanne did better with men than she did with women.

Cass had put "Tainted Love" on repeat for the last forty-minutes. Now, I couldn't tell you *exactly* why he was listening to the song again and again, but the possibility he was coming to terms with his mother killing his father was high my list.

I knew I should call Ronnie. There was a phone in Joanne's room. I could call while Cass was listening to music and he'd have no idea. But honestly, I didn't know what to say to Ronnie. It had been almost twenty-four hours since we talked. He'd be upset about that. He'd be upset that I was in Michigan. He'd still be upset that I couldn't tell him when I was coming home. I tried to think of some lies that would make him happy and calm but couldn't come up with a single one. Most of them were just as distressing as the truth.

Around eleven thirty the music stopped and Cass clumped unsteadily up the stairs, went into his bedroom, and slammed the door. Not too much later I heard him snoring. Yes, teenagers snore. Especially after they spent the evening drinking sweet and sticky liquors. I decided I should take a closer look at Joanne's walk-in closet.

Creeping down the hallway, I quietly opened the door to her room. I didn't turn on a light as there was enough streetlight slipping in through the windows. I opened the closet door and waved my hand around until I found a string that was attached to the light above me. I pulled it and the light came on. There were clothes on three sides. There wasn't a lot of floor space, just enough to easily turn around.

At first it looked like there was no real order to the way her clothes were hung. With so many things to choose from, it seemed logical to organize them either by type or color, just to be able to find things. But then I realized it was organized. She'd organized her closet by outfits. Things she liked to wear together.

I realized this when I noticed a purple leather jacket—probably the one Gavin's daughter mentioned. It hung there with a pair of black slacks, a black miniskirt, a black-and-white zebra print top, a yellow dress and unfaded designer jeans. They were all out of date. Next to them were more recent party outfits.

Opposite them were all her office clothes. She favored suits: gray, blue, black. Blouses in an array of pastel colors. No pants suits, though. For casual there were several velour tracksuits: red, green, purple.

On the floor, ringing the entire closet, were her shoes. Mostly high heels, some of them very high. All carefully lined up. The shelf above the clothes didn't hold a lot. There were a couple of spare blankets, extra pillows, a tabletop humidifier and three shoeboxes. The last stopped me. If there had been fifteen or twenty boxes it wouldn't have stopped me, I'd have assumed she kept the boxes for her shoes. But she'd only kept three. I pulled the first one down to examine. It was full of half-used makeup. There was enough makeup out on her makeup table that I couldn't see the point of keeping it, but she kept a lot of things that didn't quite make sense. I put the box aside and took down the next one.

Cash. It was full of cash. Neatly rolled in bundles with rubber bands. The bundles appeared to be mixed: twenties, fifties, hundreds. It was hard to guess how much was in there, but I'd have to go with ten, fifteen thousand. Possibly more. I wondered where it was coming from. Was it the proceeds of her credit card scams? Though that could have been in her extra bank accounts. Was it gambling money? If it was, she did well.

And why was it in cash? Why wasn't it in the bank? Was she like me? I used to have cash hidden around in case I had to make a fast exit. Did she understand her little frauds could get all her bank accounts quickly frozen? Was this her getaway fund? She could be across the border to Canada in less than an hour. At an airport in Toronto in a few hours.

I put the box back and took down the last shoe box. It held chips; a few hundred dollars' worth. They came from different casinos in Las Vegas and various other gambling towns. There were also half a dozen loyalty cards for different casino chains. I put the box back on the shelf, turned off the light, and went back to the junk room.

I got into the twin bed and stared at the ceiling. The more I found out about Joanne Di Stefano the shadier she seemed. And the more I thought it likely she was behind Dom Reilly's disappearance.

Which made me feel profoundly unsafe. If she got rid of one Dom Reilly she could get rid of another. Maybe I should just get out of bed, call a cab, and go to the airport. Let the kid do his worst. My life would be in ruins, but I'd still have a life. Or would I?

There were the crimes I'd committed as Dom Reilly. Fraud mostly. Small things that at worst could result in a few years in prison—less if

Lydia helped me. And then there were the crimes Nick Nowak had committed—or more accurately had been accused of, charged with, was wanted for. I'd skipped bail on a murder charge.

Honestly, I didn't usually think about it much. It was a long time ago and I had told the police who'd really done it. But to my knowledge the charges had never been dropped. To make that all more complicated, I'd killed the actual murderer in self-defense. Or at least I thought I had. It was dark.

No, I couldn't do it. I couldn't let this kid destroy the life I'd built. I couldn't risk going back to being Nick Nowak. I had to find a way to stay Dom Reilly.

CHAPTER ELEVEN

September 15, 1996
Sunday morning

I did finally sleep, though fitfully. I woke up around nine. It was fully light out. A peek out the window told me it was cloudy and gray. That matched my mood.

Having to empty my bladder, I stepped out into the hall. Cass's breathing was no longer a snore, but was still loud enough to hear in the hallway. I opened the door to the bathroom and stopped in my tracks.

The room was covered in vomit. It seemed to be everywhere but in the toilet. The smell was disgusting and I nearly gagged. I closed the door, went back to the junk room and got my things together, then took a shower in Joanne's bathroom. I used an old towel I found in the linen closet, one that didn't match the fluffy pink towels she had. When I was done, I took it and tossed it into the main bathroom. Cass could figure out what to do with it. Then I went downstairs and tried to find something that resembled coffee.

There was no coffeemaker, which did not come as a surprise. In a cupboard, I found a can of instant flavored coffee, sugar-free Swiss Mocha. It probably had the same amount of chemicals as a nuclear waste dump, but it also had caffeine. When I couldn't find a teapot, I boiled some water in a pan. There were plenty of cups to choose from, mostly from casinos. There was one from Lucky Days where I'd gone once. I didn't have fond memories of the place so I went with Four Queens. I followed the directions on the can and it was terrible. I added another tablespoon and it improved to simply not very good. That's when Cass walked into the room.

He looked about how you'd expect a teenager experiencing his presumably first hangover to look: pale, rumpled, a bit stunned.

"I saw what happened in the bathroom. You'd better clean that up before your mother gets home tonight."

"Why didn't you clean it up?"

"It's not my mess."

"I could make you clean it up."

"No. You couldn't."

"You need to clean the bathroom for me."

"You're forgetting I've killed three men."

"In self-defense. That's what you said."

"And what happens when you threaten me enough that it becomes self-defense?"

I couldn't believe I was threatening to kill a teenager. A child. This was not who I was, not who I wanted to be. But then again... that bathroom.

"If I wanted to kill you I could have walked into your room last night and held a pillow over your face. I didn't do that. In fact, the thought didn't even cross my mind."

"Fine. I'll clean the fucking bathroom."

As he left the room, I said, "And then we're going out for breakfast."

"Fine!"

I threw away the horrible coffee I'd made. I could wait until we got to a restaurant. There was no guarantee the coffee would be better, but I'd take my chances.

Forty-five minutes later, Cass drove me to a place called The Clock Diner that wasn't too far from his house. The booths and the chairs were covered in a mustard-colored vinyl so repulsive I couldn't believe it was ever in style. It had to have been severely discounted the last time they redecorated. Hopefully, they'd be redecorating soon.

After we were seated, I glanced at the menu. I decided on the lumberjack breakfast. I didn't even check to see what it included. I typically liked any breakfast with lumberjack in its name. Mercifully, the glum, flat-footed waitress brought coffee. And it was either very good or benefited by comparison to the swill I'd had earlier.

I ordered the lumberjack eggs over easy and Cass asked for the same. Once the waitress was gone, I said, "I want to go to your mother's office."

"Why?"

"I'd like to go through her desk."

"Do you think there will be a note in there that says 'I killed my husband'?"

"No. But there might be something that makes things clearer. I'd also like to talk to your cousins Carla and Rose."

"Why do you want to talk to them?"

"They were around when your parents got married."

"How do you know that?"

"I found your baby book. It looks like Heather gave it to your mother at her baby shower. She included a list of the people who were there."

"What else does it say?"

That was awkward. "Nothing. Your mom didn't fill out any of the pages."

Cass was quiet a moment, and then softly he said, "She was probably busy." Then he raised his voice, "What about other people?"

"What do you mean?"

"I've been thinking. What if my mother had nothing to do with it?"

"Then explain what she was doing in Reno selling your dad's identity?"

"We don't know for sure that was her. A woman in a purple coat was there. That's all the girl said."

"A woman in a purple coat with long black hair and a five-year-old."

"No. I said long black hair. You said five-year-old. She just didn't say we were wrong. So we still could be."

Great. He was paying attention. Not necessarily a good thing with a teenager. I said, "Fine. Your mother had nothing to do with it. So what do you think happened?"

"I don't know. That's what I want you to find out."

My jaw tensed and nearly bit the inside of my cheek. After exhaling slowly, I said, "Gavin said your dad got in trouble with the mob, The Partnership. That's how he ended up dead."

"He wasn't in the mob."

"He might have borrowed money from them and might not have been able to pay it back. Your parents were having money problems. Your Aunt Suzie told us that."

"Maybe," he said reluctantly.

"Was your dad active in the union? That could have gotten him into trouble."

"Maybe. I don't know," he said, brightening a bit. If organized crime killed him for resisting corruption, that would make him a hero. I could see how that might appeal to a kid

Our breakfasts arrived and were dropped in front of us. The only sounds we made for about five minutes were chewing and grunts of pleasure. When we were done, Cass burped. He tried to be subtle about it but didn't manager it. "Excuse me."

"It happens."

"So how do we prove it?"

"Prove what?"

"That my dad was killed because he was in the union."

"He wasn't killed just because he was in the union. He'd have had to be important enough to get his hands on the dues money. The Partnership would have wanted him to embezzle and give the cash to them. Something like that."

"Okay. Prove that."

My gut said this was a wild goose chase. At the far end of the building there was a pay phone on the wall.

"Do you have a quarter?"

"No."

The waitress came back and reached for our plates. Before she got her hands on them, I said, "I'll add an extra dollar to your tip if you loan us a quarter for the payphone."

She reached into the hip pocket of her uniform and pulled out a change purse. She picked out a quarter and put in on the table in front of me. Then she snatched up the plates, saying, "I'll bring your check."

I slid the quarter over to Cass. "Call your Aunt Suzie. Ask her if your father ever held any offices in the union."

"Why don't you do it?"

"For one thing, I don't think she trusts me. And for another you need to hear this yourself."

Cass got out of the booth and slunk back to the pay phone. I sat there wishing for a refill on my coffee. The waitress brought the check, I asked for a refill on the coffee, then took my credit card out to pay the bill.

I was about half way through my refilled cup of coffee when Cass came back to the booth.

"How'd it go?"

"She asked a lot of questions about you. She called Big Brothers and found out they don't help kids find their parents."

"Yeah. I didn't think she bought it. What did you tell her?"

"I said I was using the money I made on weekends to pay you."

"Did she buy that?"

"No. I had to tell her I borrowed some money from my mom's gambling stash."

I didn't have to ask if she bought that. I was sure she would. I wondered how many people knew about the money Joanne kept in her closet. I also wondered if that really was a gambling stash. Was she that good at it? Of course, if she was pretty enough and clever enough she might not ever have to stake herself in a casino, which would make walking out with cash a lot more likely.

And then I realized there were no photos in their house. None of Cass and none of Joanne. The only thing on their walls were a couple of paintings. The kind you bought in a furniture store when you picked out your sofa.

"What did she say about the union?" I asked.

"She said my dad paid his dues. And that was it."

The waitress came back with my credit card and the slip to sign. I made good on my promise to tip her extra for the quarter. She looked like she might smile but then seemed to decide it was too much effort.

I looked at Cass and said, "Shall we?"

In the car it seemed like he might resist going to Top Dawg, but he gave up before he started and we silently drove there. It was located in what was probably called an office park. A wide, two-story brick building with mirrored windows that reflected the large parking lot. There were several like that, all in a row.

Before we got out of the car, Cass put the anti-theft bar onto his steering wheel. Something that seemed pointless since there were only a few other cars in the lot. We walked over to the glass and steel entrance. The doors were open and we walked past a security desk. There was a clipboard sitting on the counter where we were probably supposed to sign in, but there was no security guard at that moment so we didn't bother.

We took the elevator to the second floor, where we walked down a winding hallway until we got to office number 225. There was a plaque next to the door that said: TOP DOG COLLECTIONS.

Right away that was a problem. The stationery Joanne used at home said Top Dawg. D-A-W-G. What was going on? Was she syphoning off accounts to her similar sounding company? Top Dog would buy the debt and then Top Dawg would collect it? Is that how it worked? Did she mark them down as uncollectible and then bring them home? She had to have a way to get them off the Top Dog books…

Cass got out his keys and opened the door. Immediately, we were in a small outer office with a desk and a row of filing cabinets. Behind that were two doors to separate offices: One said ANTON CRAY, ESQ, the other JOANNE DI STEFANO, CP.

At the desk sat a young Black woman with carefully braided hair, a significant amount of colorful jewelry and expertly manicured nails. She was on the phone with a stack of files spread out in front of her.

"I'm gonna have to call you back. No, I will call you back. Yes, I will. Yes—" Apparently, she was hung up on. With a frown she set down the phone. "Well, hello Mr. Cass. What are you doing here on a Sunday?"

The boy was obviously tongue-tied, so I said, "His mother forgot something in her desk."

"Did she now. And you are?"

"A friend of the family," I said, hoping she didn't know the family too well.

She didn't pursue that but instead said, "Sometimes I come in on Sundays and do calls. Deadbeats think we take weekends off so they answer their phones."

I had the feeling there was more to it than that. Probably something dodgy. Probably not as dodgy as what Joanne had going, but who knew. I was getting the impression that squeezing pennies out of broke people was so profitable that Anton Cray didn't have to worry much about his employees opening their own revenue streams.

"We'll leave you to it, then," I said. I nodded at Cass to get him to lead me to his mother's office. He popped to life and led me into the office.

The office had a window that looked out onto a wooded area. There was the desk with a computer sitting on it, a credenza behind it, a guest chair, a bookcase filled with three-inch binders, and a corn plant that was thriving. On the wall was an idyllic scene of a cabin in the woods.

"Who is that?" I whispered.

"Claudia. She's the secretary."

"Does she normally make collection calls?"

He shrugged.

"Find something we can say we came to get. Something personal," I said, then I went and sat behind the desk. I started opening the drawers.

Obviously, I didn't expect to find anything to do with Joanne's embezzling from Top Dog. She kept all evidence of that at home. What I was looking for was more personal. Something she might want to hide from Cass.

The desk top was neat. There was a spotless blotter, a computer that looked recent—but then what did I know—a telephone that matched the one Claudia was using, with lights on the side that showed which lines were in use, a cup from Caesar's Palace filled with pens, in and out trays with neat stacks of paper, and a box of tissues.

One of the lights on the phone came on. Claudia was on the phone again. I listened a moment. While I couldn't hear exactly what she was saying, I heard the words lawsuit, garnish and judgement. Another collection call.

I glanced at Cass. He was completely still, yet tense. Like he was waiting for a bomb to go off. I didn't have time to deal with him. The top drawer held paperclips, a stapler, a couple of rubber stamps, a roll of US stamps—thirty-two cents, yellow roses, Post-its, some spare change, a bottle of clear nail polish and a random pink lipstick.

The drawer on the left held business envelopes and small lined pads. The drawer on my right held a deposit bag for Chase Manhattan. I took it out and flipped through. There were about twenty checks equaling close to thirty thousand dollars. They were all made out to TOP DOG COLLECTIONS and dated in the last week. If that was an average weekly haul, then I could see why it was so simple for Cray's employees to help themselves to a bit off the top.

When I put the bag back into the drawer my hand brushed against something in the back. I pulled it out. A photograph. Polaroid. There was a pretty teenage girl with a big smile and black hair done up in high pigtails like the girl in *Three's Company*. Next to her was a muscular guy around the same age with curly black hair, a crisp jawline and a permanent five o'clock shadow. He had an arm slung over the girl in a possessive way. His dark eyes seemed to challenge all comers.

I'd already noticed there were no photos at the house, and no photo albums that I'd been able to find. So why did Joanne have this photo? Why was it here? In her desk?

I showed it to Cass, asking, "Do you know who these people are?"

"Yeah. That's my mom."

"And the guy?"

"My second cousin, Luca."

CHAPTER TWELVE

September 15, 1996
Sunday afternoon

It wasn't hard leaving the office, Claudia was deep into a call, "Don't you have any family? Can't you ask your mother for the money? Your dad? You have a brother? You have friends, don't you? You really need to pay this bill. The doctor saved your life, and you owe—I see. I see. Well, I'm sure he did his best by you. And medical school isn't free, you know."

Once the door was shut behind us, I asked Cass, "Do you know how all of that works?"

"I already told you."

"Tell me again."

"There's these companies that buy debt from department stores and hospitals and places. Like, people can't pay and they don't feel like making them pay. So these other companies buy up lots of that bad debt. Pennies on the dollar. Then Mr. Cray buys it from them for a tiny bit more than they paid. He only buys debt in Michigan in case he needs to go to court. Mostly they threaten people a bunch of times until they cough up some money, so he doesn't go to court a lot."

"Sweet," I said sarcastically.

By the time he was done, we were climbing into his car.

"How long have you worked there?"

"Since I was fifteen."

"That's young."

"It's not hard."

Yeah, screwing over poor people never is.

He unlocked the anti-theft bar and took it off the steering wheel, turned the key and pressed the button that put the car in reverse. We were on our way.

Carla and Rose Amato were both still single. They lived together in a two-story, white clapboard house just outside the Eastern Market area. The neighborhood had seen better times, but their house was well-kept. Neat and clean.

One of them answered the door, I wasn't sure which. She was just passed forty, had coal black hair that might have been dyed, very pale skin and eyes like a cornered cat. She wore a gray pants suit with a pale peach blouse underneath, and smelled of three or four mismatched beauty products. She'd obviously just come from church.

"Hey Carla," the boy said, standing slightly behind me.

"Well, hello Cassidy. What are you doing here?"

"I want to find out what happened to my dad."

"We have no idea. If we did we'd have said so by now."

"You might be able to set us in the right direction," I said. "If we could come in, just for a few minutes."

"And you are?"

"I'm a private detective. I'm not charging Cass. I'm doing this pro bono." Not what he'd told his aunt, but whatever.

"Isn't that big of you. Do you have a card?"

"In my other jeans."

And then her sister was behind her. "Carla, what's happening?"

Rose looked younger than her sister, had dark brown hair and eyes to match. Her skin was every bit as pale as Carla's.

"They want to talk about Dominick."

"All right. Carla, move over so they can get in. There's no reason to be unfriendly. We don't have anything to hide. Do we?"

The women stepped aside and we were immediately in a small living room with a couple of reclining chairs and an old gray sofa. Beyond the living room was an open dining room with a nice wooden table and six chairs.

"There's coffee," Rose said. "We always have coffee after church." Then she scooted out of the room.

We stood uncomfortably, until Carla finally said, "Well, sit down then." She gestured toward the dining room table. As I sat at one end of the table, Carla sat at the other while saying, "I don't know what you think you're going to find out. I can't say we knew Dominick all that well. He wasn't popular with our family."

"And why was that?"

"Well, he was a Mick for one thing. That's what my grandfather would have said. It's not a term I use often."

"He didn't like the Irish?"

"Hated them. No, no one was happy when Dominick and Joanne got married. She could have done worse, of course. My family hates coloreds and wetbacks more than Micks. A lot of girls back then, well... not that it would have mattered."

"Was that the only thing wrong with Dominick?"

"Joanne didn't help things. She was always complaining about him. He wasn't ambitious enough or smart enough or good-looking enough or basically anything enough."

"What did you think?"

"I thought Joanne was a brat. Her expectations weren't exactly in line with reality. I'm sorry Cass, but that's what I thought."

The boy shrugged. I suspected it was still what she thought.

"What can you tell me about Joanne's relationship with your brother Luca."

Then Rose was back. She carried a tray that had a pot of coffee, cups, a bottle of powdered coffee creamer and a small plate of store-bought lemon cookies. As she set the tray down, she said to Cass, "If I'd known you and your friend were coming I'd have baked cookies. These aren't terrible, but I love to do extra when we have company. Don't I, Carla?"

"They're asking about Joanne and Luca."

Rose stopped for just a moment, took a short breath, then set the cups around. "I brought out creamer. We didn't know you were coming or I would have bought real cream. It's an indulgence but worth it. Not that we mind people stopping by. It's always nice when people stop by. They don't very often, but still..."

The cups were placed and she began to pour the coffee.

"It's Eight O'Clock. The coffee, not the time. I get it at Farmer Jack. The one that used to be an A&P. They have the best prices, I think. Help yourself to the coffee creamer. It's sweet so you don't need sugar."

"I take my coffee black," I said.

Cass reached for the creamer.

"Help yourself to a cookie then," Rose said. "They're store brand but really not too bad. I like to bake when people—"

"You told us, Rose."

"Oh. Of course, I did."

She'd poured everyone's coffee so she sat down. Then she took a cookie. Staring at her coffee she said, "We don't like talking about Luca."

"Can you tell me why?"

"That would be talking about Luca," Carla pointed out.

I knew I was going to have to nibble around the edges before they'd say anything about him. "What about the rest of your family? Tell us about them."

Carla studied me for a moment. I figured she knew exactly what I was up to, so it was a question of what she really wanted to tell me. After a long moment, she said, "My father always told us family is everything, but it was really just a way to get us to do what he wanted."

"Luca's the boy. He gets everything," Rose said.

"So you're not on good terms with your mom and dad?"

"We're not." The way Carla said it made it sound like it was a point of pride It also sounded final, like she wanted to close the subject.

"We take care of ourselves," Rose said. "Carla works as an accountant for a company that makes mufflers. I do temporary secretarial work. Now and then."

I took a sip of coffee, it wasn't bad, and reached for a cookie. I was hoping that if I remained quiet one of them, Rose in particular, would keep talking.

"Luca was in prison," Rose said.

Carla added, "Assault."

"How long was he in prison?"

"Two years."

There was more to it than that. In most states a first-time simple assault was a misdemeanor that would likely get you a fine, restitution and probation. Two years in prison meant multiple offenses or he caused serious injury to someone. Or both.

"When was that?" I asked.

"Eighty-seven, eighty-eight."

That meant he'd have been around to get rid of Dom in 1982. I asked, "Joanne and Luca were always close?"

Rose nodded, "My grandmother used to say they'd have gotten married in the old country."

"Do you think there was something romantic going on between them?"

Rose paled. And then her sister stepped in, "Just kid stuff. Spin the bottle. That kind of thing."

"How old is Luca?"

"He's in between Rose and I. Thirty-seven."

A few years older than Joanne. That would have been significant when they were teenagers. Not so much as adults.

"Is he married?"

"He's never married," Carla said. "He lives with our parents."

I wondered if that had anything to do with why they didn't. I said, "You've heard the rumors, I assume."

"Which rumor?" Carla asked, her voice going hard. "The rumor that Luca is in The Partnership? Or that he got rid of Dominick for Joanne?"

"Either."

"Life is never as exciting as people want it to be," she said, though it really wasn't an answer. "My father isn't involved with organized crime. He'd like people to think he is, but he's not. And our brother is a pretty average guy. As long as he doesn't get mad at you, he can be really sweet."

I noticed Rose staring at her coffee as though it might bite her.

"What was it like when Dominick disappeared?" I asked.

"What do you mean?"

"Were people upset, angry... How did everyone react?"

"His family was upset, of course. They never believed he'd just run off."

"Joanne was happy," Rose said, looking up from her coffee. "She said her life could start now that he was gone. It was... unseemly."

"It was," Carla said dryly.

There was a lot going on in this branch of the Di Stefano family. Particularly for poor Rose. Something that had to do with Luca. The parents had chosen Luca and Carla had chosen her sister. The question was, did it have anything to do with Dominick's disappearance? I wasn't sure.

"Would you like more coffee?" Rose asked.

Cass started to say yes, but I said, "No. I think we need to move on. You've been helpful. Thank you for talking to us."

And then I was standing. Cass followed suit and the women walked us out. At the door, Rose pulled Cass close, and said, "You need to visit more. Next time I'll make cookies."

"Okay," he said, unconvincingly.

Once we were in Cass's car, he asked, "So what are we doing now?"

"Logically we should follow your cousin Luca around to get a feel for what he's up to. You should have let me rent a car."

"What's wrong with my car?"

"It draws attention. If you're following someone you don't want to do that."

"Why not just talk to him?"

"Sure, we can go ask if he killed your dad. He'll say no, but when he kills one of us we'll know he lied."

"Don't talk to me like I'm stupid."

"Don't ask stupid questions."

We sat there quietly for a few minutes. Then I asked, "What about your mother's sisters? Should we talk to them?"

"My Aunt Josette works at an Italian bakery on McNichols."

I had no idea where that was, but it sounded like it might be far away. I reached into my jeans pocket and took out the slip of paper Suzie had given me with Dickie Potter's number on it.

"Find a pay phone."

"You could ask Carla if we could—"

"We don't want them to know what we're doing, do we?"

"But... Okay."

It took five minutes to find a pay phone at a gas station. Using my calling card, I called the number and spoke to Dickie's belligerent wife who told me he was, as usual, at The Corktown Social Club, and that if I saw him I should tell him to 'go fuck himself.' Then I called 411 and got the address.

The Corktown Social Club was located in an old wooden building sitting on a corner with its name painted on the side in shamrock green. The second floor had some nice windows and looked like there might be an apartment or two up there. Cass parked across the street, and said, "I'm coming in with you."

"You're seventeen."

"I'm not going to order a drink, okay?"

"You think he'll tell me more or less with you sitting there?"

He struggled with that. I could tell he was trying to find a way to say we'd learn more, but before he could I got out of the car and ran over to the bar.

Inside, the bar was furnished like a VFW hall with banquet-style chairs and tables. The coolers behind the bar were covered in sports stickers. A TV sat on a shelf in the corner up by the ceiling. A ceiling that was painted over pressed-tin, suggesting a more elegant past.

There were about eight men sitting at the bar, only one of them was under sixty. I walked over to the guy. He was in his early forties, bald and thick around the middle. There was a flush in his cheeks that suggested he spent a lot of time in bars.

"Dickie Potter?"

"Who are you?"

"I'm a friend of Cass Reilly's."

"You're a friend of a kid? What is he now, twelve?"

"Seventeen? He's asked me to look into his father's disappearance."

"So, what? You're like a private detective for the Hardy boys?"

Rude, but I decided to ignore it. "Yeah, pretty much. Can you tell me about your friendship with Dominick Reilly?"

The bartender came over. I ordered a draft just to be polite and threw a few bucks on the bar. I ordered a refill for Dickie and a shot of whatever he liked. He liked Bushmills.

When he was all set up he said, "Dominick and I went to school together. For most of it. His family moved to Roseville when we were fourteen, fifteen. Somewhere in there. But we kept up, you know. My family moved out that way in nineteen seventy."

"But you moved back?"

"Kind of. I have a house in Roseville, but I bought one down here a couple years back. Didn't cost anything. Now I'm fixing it up."

I couldn't see how that required sitting in a bar, but I didn't say anything.

"Are you into cars?" I prompted. "The way Dominick was?"

"Oh, yeah."

"What do you have?"

"I've got a sixty-six Dodge Charger. Baby blue. One of the first off the line. 426 Hemi. Four-speed. Everything on it is mint."

"You ever hear what happened to Dominick's Barracuda?"

He shook his head. "My guess is it's in Lake St. Clair or Lake Erie with Dominick sitting in the front seat. At least I hope they're together."

"So you don't think he'd just had enough and ran off?"

"No. He loved Joanne. And the kid. He loved Cass."

"Who do you think killed him?"

"Joanne was cheating on him. I know that."

"With her cousin?"

"No. I mean, maybe but... Dominick didn't know about that. He only knew about the lawyer."

"The one she works for now?"

"Yeah. I think that's the one."

Could that be true? Was that why she wanted to become a paralegal? Was that also why Dominick wanted her to hold off on it?

"Does Suzie know this?"

"I never wanted to tell her. She doesn't need to know that her brother was just some chump whose wife was cheating on him. And..."

"And what?"

"I was afraid of what she might do."

"What did you think she might do?"

"When we were kids she was always getting into fights. Beat the crap out of one kid who called me and Dominick faggots cause we were friends. Just made things worse. Having your sister beat-up a bully. It was a good thing when they moved to Roseville."

"She still like that? Beating people up?"

"Naw, I don't think so. I'm talking about the sixties. It was a lot more common for people to beat each other up."

"Yeah, I remember. Did Dominick plan on doing anything about the affair?"

Dickie made a raspberry sound. "He made excuses for her. She was young, she didn't know better, her family treated her badly and it was their fault she didn't understand right and wrong."

"I've heard rumors her family is involved in organized crime. Any truth to that?"

"I would say there's a lot of truth to it."

"And you know that because?"

"Because everybody knows it. Her father, her uncle, her cousin... they're all involved. Nothing big, just this and that. Small time stuff. You're not from around here, are you?"

"I'm not. No."

"So you think someone in Joanne's family killed Dominick?"

"I do."

"Do you have any proof?"

"If I had proof I wouldn't tell you or anyone else. This is a situation where proof can get you killed. And I think that's all I'm going to say."

I put a five on the bar and stood up.

"Thanks. You told me a lot. And by the way, I talked to your wife on the phone. She said you should go fuck yourself."

He smiled wryly. "Can you believe I married her because she was so sweet?"

CHAPTER THIRTEEN

September 15, 1996
Sunday evening

W hen we pulled up in front of Cass's house there was a recent
model silver 5-series BMW sitting in front. It was close to
seven and I was getting pretty hungry.

"That's Mr. Cray," Cass said, and I realized I wouldn't be eating
dinner any time soon.

We pulled into the driveway. I looked back at the BMW. I hadn't realized at first, but there were two people sitting inside the car. A gray-haired
man in the drivers' seat and a woman with a lot of black hair. After a
moment, she leaned over the seat and kissed him on the cheek. Then she
got out of the car and he drove off.

Joanne Di Stefano gave the impression of being tall—that was likely
because of her hairstyle, which added two or three inches above her head,
and her heels which added another three inches. She wobbled across a strip
of grass and then was on the sidewalk.

Her hair was pitch black and probably included a fall or two—no one
seemed to have told her the eighties were over. I couldn't see her eyes as
they were behind a giant pair of sunglasses. She wore a mink jacket which
just begged for someone to throw red paint on it, and beneath that a deep

purple, form-fitting dress. Around her neck was a gold necklace that said JOANNE in a pretty script. She had a designer purse hooked in one elbow and an expensive looking travel bag hanging from her other hand.

When she saw Cass get out of the Belvedere, she dropped the bag, threw her arms in the air and screamed, "There's my baby! Oh my God I missed you." She picked her way up the driveway until she got to Cass and pulled him into a tight embrace.

He seemed to resist for a moment—possibly because of all the times I'd mentioned that his mother might have had his father killed—but then he gave in to her embrace. She was kissing him all over his face when I got out of the car.

She stopped abruptly, and asked, "Who the fuck are you?"

"He's a friend of mine," Cass said.

"When did you start having middle-aged friends?" Then to me. "If you touched my son—"

"Mom, that's so gross."

"Then who is he? Who are you?"

"I'm Dom Reilly."

She looked me up and down, and asked, "Is that some kind of joke? Cause mister you got a funny sense of humor."

"You went to Reno sometime between 1982 and 1986 and sold your husband's identity to a guy named Gavin. I bought it."

She looked at Cass for a long beat, then said to me, "You're saying that kind of shit to me on my front lawn? My own fucking front lawn?"

"Mom."

"Go get my bag," she snapped at her son, then she went up to the house and let herself in. Cass walked down to the sidewalk and got her bag. I dawdled. I assumed I was supposed to follow them into the house but didn't want to go first.

At the door, Cass said, "Come on. It's okay."

"It doesn't seem okay."

He shrugged and went into the house. I followed him. Inside, Joanne had shrugged her way out of the mink jacket and was standing in the living room with her hands on her hips. "Okay. Okay, so fucking what?"

"Mom."

"Shut up. Yeah, so I sold some old paperwork to a guy in Reno. Big deal. And by the way, people like that are supposed to have confidentiality."

"Yeah, I don't think Gavin's a lawyer."

She shrugged like it was an unimportant point. "How is Gavin, since we're talking about him?"

"He went to prison and then he died."

"So, not good."

"His daughter remembers your purple leather coat."

"That's sweet of her. I love that coat. I still have it. I should wear it more often."

"Did you kill your husband?"

"What the fuck? Of course not." She fidgeted a moment, then said, "Let's go out to the patio." She grabbed her purse and led us through the house to the patio.

I watched Cass. He seemed to relax when she said she didn't kill her husband. I didn't believe her, but I could tell he did. Or at least wanted to. When we got to the patio, I was happy to find the sun had come out from behind the clouds.

Even though it was in the low sixties, it felt warmer. Frigid in California but cheery and warm in the Midwest. Joanne plunked her purse on her lap and dug around until she found a pack of long, skinny cigarettes and a matching lighter. As she lit her cigarette, I asked, "You don't smoke inside?"

"Are you kidding? I spent a fortune on those drapes. Wouldn't ever get the smell of smoke out of them." She exhaled as dramatically as she could then said, "Look, we were in a lot of financial trouble. Dominick wasn't working much and we were broke. He took a loan from the wrong people and when they couldn't collect... I was told they were just going to rough him up, you know encourage him to find the money, and they sort of over did it."

"How come you never told me that?" Cass asked.

"You're a kid. You don't tell a kid his father was a dumb ass who got himself killed cause he couldn't manage money. What kind of mother would do that?"

I felt offended for the poor guy. "How much of what he owed was money you gambled away?"

"Dominick liked to gamble, too. Don't try to make it my fault. My luck is always good."

No one else had said Dominick liked to gamble, but I let it pass. It might be true, though I suspected it wasn't.

"So why did you get rid of his stuff and pretend he disappeared?"

"Because I got a phone call and that's what they told me to do."

"But you kept his important papers."

"I don't throw away things that are valuable."

"Why didn't you ever have him declared dead? You could have gotten social security benefits for your son."

"Crumbs. I don't go out of my way for crumbs."

That didn't fit with saving his papers and then selling them for what was probably much less than she could have gotten for her kid. But I could tell Cass was eating this up, believing every word.

It wasn't all that surprising when he asked, "Do you know the name of the guy who killed Dad?"

"Oh yeah, sure. Some loan shark is going to call me up and tell me so-and-so beat your husband to death, because that's how this works. Sorry about that."

"So who did tell you?" I asked.

"What do you mean?"

"You said you were told they were just going to rough up your husband but then overshot the mark. Who told you that?"

To Cass she said, "Baby, go get your mother a vodka on the rocks. Grey Goose." Which explained the boys familiarity with the liquor cabinet. As soon as he was in the house, she crushed out her cigarette on the concrete patio, and asked, "What the fuck are you doing here?"

"Your son flew out to California and found me, threatened to blow up my life if I didn't help him find whoever killed his father. I'm here under duress."

"Huh. I guess he's not the spineless little wimp I thought he was."

"Yeah. Good parenting works," I said dryly. "You're making up this story about your husband getting beaten to death by accident, aren't you?"

She took a good look at me, and said, "You're a faggot aren't you? I clocked you right away. You wanna know how?"

"Not really."

"Don't worry. You're not the obvious sort. Most people wouldn't suspect you. It's just that men, real men, react to me in a particular way. You didn't."

Cass was back with his mother's drink.

"I was just telling your mother how you and I met."

The boy had the decency to blush.

"All we need is the name of the guy who accidentally killed your dad and then I can go home."

"Well, I'm sure I don't know it," Joanne said.

"We could start with who told you—"

"Wait a minute." She looked at Cass and asked, "Who paid for you to fly to California? And who paid for you to fly back here?"

"I paid for the trip to Reno," I said. "And the flight back here. But that's not what's most important."

"Where are you staying? Is there a rental car out front? I didn't see one."

"He staying in the junk room," Cass said. "And I've been driving him around," Cass said.

"Well, you're going to have to leave. You can't stay here."

"Mom—"

"Don't Mom me. It's my house. You don't get to have overnight guests. Particularly middle-aged faggots." She stood up and added, "I'm going to take a shower. When I come back he's going to be gone." Then she walked into the house.

It didn't escape me that she'd avoided answering the question of who'd told her Dominick was 'accidentally' beaten to death. I could have tried again for an answer, but it was clear she didn't have one.

Cass looked at me sheepishly, and said, "Sorry. I'll go grab your stuff."

There was no reason for me to be there anymore, so I didn't see the point of worrying about a few pairs of underwear and some Tylenol.

"Why don't you just drive me to the airport?"

"You're not done! We don't know who killed my dad."

"Your mom said it was an accident." Yeah, so I didn't believe that, but I had to try to get out of there. "Why can't you leave it at that?"

"It's not okay to beat people to death by accident, is it?"

"No. It's not. Am I supposed to sleep on the lawn?"

"There's a Motel 6 out on 10 Mile Road. You can use my car." He reached into his pocket and pulled out the keys and gave them to me. Then he handed me a wad of paper. I took it and unfolded it.

Inside was a credit card in the name of Charles Henderson. A VISA.

"What is this for?"

"You spent a lot of money on airplane tickets."

"So you thought you'd implicate me in fraud?"

"That's how I got to LA."

The pieces of paper were a temporary driver's license for Mr. Henderson and a police report describing how his wallet got stolen.

"These are fakes, right?"

"They work."

To be honest, they were pretty good. His mother had taught him well. I decided I would borrow the car but wouldn't use the credit card. I took it anyway though, just so we could stop talking about it.

"Go up to 10 Mile Road and head east. You'll see the signs for Motel 6. I'll call you in the morning."

"Goody."

INTERLUDE

Summer 1982

Frank Sinatra sang "My Way" on a juke box somewhere. The young couple was seated at a small table in the center of the room. It was still early so the restaurant was half empty. The waiter, who was well into his fifties and wore a gigantic white apron, brought over a bottle of Valpolicella and a single glass.

"We need two glasses."

"I'll need to see the young lady's ID."

She had long black hair which she wore parted down the middle and ironed. She flipped one side over her shoulder and set her purse on her lap. Carefully opening the purse, her nails were quite long and painted red, she took out her wallet saying, "It's my twenty-first birthday. Legal at last."

"And your boyfriend brought you out for dinner. What a nice fellow."

"Husband," she said flatly while handing the waiter her license.

After glancing at it, the waiter said, "I'll get you a glass."

"Can I get a martini? Straight up with a lemon twist. *And* a glass."

"Of course. Gin or vodka?"

The girl blushed as her husband said, "Smirnoff." When the waiter was gone, she carefully opened her cloth napkin and set it on her lap. "When I was a little girl I'd hear my parents order martinis. I thought they'd be sweet, like a dessert. Then my father let me try one. It wasn't sweet. But I liked it anyway."

"Go easy. I've only got seventy bucks."

"Don't worry, Dominick. I've got money."

That was a humiliating thought. His wife paying for her own birthday dinner. And... he didn't know where the money had come from. He gave her an allowance, but she always seemed to spend more than he'd given her and always had cash on hand. He assumed the extra money came from her family, but he didn't dare think about it much.

"Can I have my present?"

"You don't want to wait until dessert?"

"No. I want it now."

From the house to the car to the restaurant, he'd kept the wrapped box hidden in his folded coat. He'd bought her a scarf, silk, colorful and large. It had cost almost thirty dollars—more than they could afford. But he knew she'd love it, it was mostly purple.

When he slipped the box out from its hiding place, she said, "That's too big."

"You haven't opened it yet."

"It's not what I wanted."

He sighed. "I know what you wanted, Joanne, but I'm not working. I have to pay the rent, we have to eat."

"We've been married more than three years. I think I deserve an engagement ring."

"I didn't say you don't deserve it. I said I can't afford it."

"This isn't what I wanted."

"Open it. You might like it anyway."

"I didn't mean the cruddy present. I meant *this*."

"Maybe it's not what I wanted either. But it's what we have."

"You think I should have gotten rid of him."

"I didn't say that. When did I say that? I love the kid."

"If you really loved the kid you'd try harder to make me happy."

He struggled with the sense of that for a moment, then he asked a question that had been bothering him for a long time. "Why did you fight so hard to have him? Most of the time it seems like you don't want him around."

There wasn't time to answer. The waiter was back with her martini and an empty glass for wine. When he asked if they were ready to order Dominick said they'd wait.

"But bring us a shrimp cocktail," Joanne added.

"Of course," the waiter said before drifting off.

Dominick had been watching his wife's neck. Beneath the collar of her lavender top there was a flash of gold. It had been distracting him since they got into the car. It looked like it was real gold. Not that he had much experience, but you didn't have to be a jeweler to recognize quality.

"Where'd you get the chain?"

"Bought it."

"Let me see it."

"I said I bought it."

"Yeah, so let me see it."

She pulled it over the collar of her blouse. It said JOANNE in script.

"Somebody gave that to you."

"No. I bought it."

"You didn't buy it."

"Okay. Fine. I stole it. It's not hard."

"You're shoplifting? You've got a baby, you can't get yourself arrested!"

"I didn't get arrested. I told you, it's not hard."

"You could have gotten arrested."

"I wanted it so I took it. What's the big deal?"

"Are you going to teach our son to steal?"

"I'm going to teach him how to get what he wants."

CHAPTER FOURTEEN

September 16, 1996
Monday morning

The less said about Motel 6 the better. It was your basic two-story corporate hotel. The room was bare and clean. There was a queen-sized bed with a mattress that was a bit lumpy and sheets that had a thread count of about thirty. The best thing I could think of to say about the place was that Norman Bates didn't work there.

I'd slept well. Mostly because I hadn't the night before. And there was the advantage of not having a teenager around to throw up all over the bathroom. I was dreaming that I was being crushed by some malevolent enemy, when the phone started to ring and saved me. I sat on the edge of the bed for a minute, trying to calm the pain in my shoulder. It wasn't quite gone when I picked up. "Yeah?"

"I told you to use the card I gave you."

"I decided to use my own card."

"I asked for Charles Henderson. I thought you might have run off."

"I'd like to run off."

"You have to take me to school."

"I have to take you to school?"

"Yeah, I'm in high school, remember?"

"How about playing hooky?"

"My mom freaked out when I said I was staying home. And they call her if I don't show up."

It sounded like he might have some experience with that. I asked, "Why doesn't *she* drive you to school? That way she'll know you're there."

"Just come get me. Jesus Christ."

And then he hung up.

I took a very hot shower wishing I'd told him to bring my Tylenol with him. Then I got dressed in yesterday's clothes. The red turtleneck—now on its third day—and the blue crew neck sweater. I looked very patriotic. Didn't matter, though. I was hoping I'd get to fly home later in the day.

I made my way back to their house pretty easily. Cass was standing in front of the house with the backpack he'd used to travel across country slung over his shoulder. He climbed into the Belvedere.

"You'll have to direct me. I don't know where your high school is."

"Go straight." Then he directed me back out to 10 Mile Road.

"So you're a senior?" I asked.

"Yeah. What did you think? I got held back?"

"It was just a question. Are you thinking of going to college?"

"Like my mom's going to send me to college. She already told me I have to get out as soon as I graduate."

"Well that's not very maternal."

I'd already figured out that maternal wasn't exactly Joanne's jam.

"Says you. My mom was married with a baby when she was seventeen. There's nothing wrong with growing up."

"You know your mom is quite the character."

"I love my mom. And she loves me."

"Yeah, you're a match made in heaven."

We rode along quietly for a minute or two.

"Did your mother say anything of value after I left?"

He looked out his window, watching the lovely suburban neighborhood go by. Then he shrugged, "She yelled at me for using one of her credit cards."

"Did she figure out you gave one to me?"

"No. It's safe to use it."

"I'm not— You do know that stealing is wrong, don't you?"

"Stealing from credit card companies isn't wrong. I mean, they're trying to steal from us. It's just fighting back."

I decided to leave that one alone. A moment later he asked, "So, like, what are you going to do today?"

"You said you have an aunt who works at a bakery. I thought I'd go talk to her."

"You should talk to Luca. He's probably the one who told my mom that someone accidentally killed my dad."

"It sounds like he's dangerous whether he did it or not," I pointed out.

"You told me you killed three men. I think you'll be all right."

I should never brag. There was a time when I wouldn't have hesitated to go talk to someone connected to organized crime. I'd done it quite a lot in Chicago. I'd known it was dangerous when I did it and I hadn't cared. Now I had a lot more to lose, and not just my own life. The lives of those around me.

For instance, this kid. I could get him killed if I wasn't careful. He was stubborn, difficult and obnoxious. Which didn't mean I wanted to see him dead.

"You want me to kill him for you? Is that what you're angling for?"

"No. I want to kill him."

I wondered if he'd be able to. Under the right circumstances anyone can be a killer. Or at least that's what they say. So I guess the question was, were these the right circumstances for Cass?

The high school was a two-story, blond brick building sitting in the middle of a massive parking lot. There was a line of cars waiting to drop kids off.

"What is this?" I asked. "Doesn't anyone take a bus anymore?"

"Poor kids take the bus."

I decided not to break it to him that if his mother tried to live on what she earned he'd be one of the poor kids.

Before he got out of the car, he said, "School's out at three. Pick me up."

I drove around for quite some time trying to find a cup of coffee. I was navigating via 10 Mile Road which seemed to be the big conduit in this area. I drove by a lot of green, empty fields and backyards until I finally found an intersection with a Walgreens and a bank branch on two of the four corners. One of the other corners had a gas station with a minimart attached. I walked in and found that I was lucky. Sort of.

I poured a large cup of coffee, picked out a tin of twelve Tylenol, and was about to risk a mass-produced cinnamon roll when I remember something. I put the roll down and went up to the counter with my coffee. As the clerk was checking me out, I asked, "I'm looking for an Italian bakery on McNichols."

"Four eighty-three," he said.

I gave him a five. He handed me seventeen cents, then said, "Keep on 10 Mile until you get to Telegraph then go south to McNichols, just after the cemetery."

"Okay. Thanks."

As soon as I got back into the Belvedere I realized I had a problem. There was no such thing as a cupholder in 1958. I sat at the gas station, swallowed four Tylenol and drank my coffee until I was halfway through it.

The car also didn't have a clock. I figured it was a pretty basic model. Problem was I never wear a watch so I had to guess at the time. I'd dropped Cass off around eight, spent a lot of time driving down 10 Mile Road, and been sipping coffee for at least ten minutes. It had to be around nine.

I got out and tossed the rest of my coffee into a garbage can, then got back in and set off for the bakery on McNichols. About ten minutes later I'd found Telegraph and then completely missed the turn onto McNichols. I doubled back and started going east looking for an Italian bakery.

I found it about six blocks from Telegraph. It was called Barones and had a red-green-and-white awning. Signs in the window advertised that they were open, and that they served cannolis and cakes as well as imported Italian specialty foods. The building was free-standing and there was parking along the sides.

When I walked in a bell rang above my head. I was met by a row of glass cases filled with cookies, pastries and cakes. Behind the cases, a woman in her early sixties stood frowning at me. Her hair was gray, refused to be pulled back, and her eyes suspicious. She wore a smudged apron.

I busied myself looking at all the cookies. I pointed and asked, "Can I get a dozen of these?"

"Biscotti originali?"

"Yeah, thanks."

Using her hands, she plunked a dozen in a white bag. Before she was finished, I asked, "So... is Josette Di Stefano working today?"

She stood up, looked around the small shop as if she might find Josette, then said, "No. She's not."

"Do you know Josette well?"

"Who are you?"

"Name's Chuck Henderson."

Why not? I could almost prove it.

"I'm helping out Josette's nephew, Cass Reilly. He wants to know what happened to his father."

"He's not the only one."

"Did you know Dominick Reilly?"

"We went to Saint Rose for a while. His family went there, too. They said a mass for Dominick at least once a year."

I wondered if my family ever had a mass said for me. Then I quickly pushed away the idea. It didn't matter. I was fine. I wasn't in a car at the bottom of Lake Erie.

"Do you think he just ran off?"

She shrugged and said, "Men do, you know."

"What does Josette think?"

"She and her sister aren't close. Mainly because her sister's a narcissistic whore." Before I could ask, she added, "Her words. Not mine. Not that I disagree."

"Does she think her sister had Dominick killed?"

"She doesn't have any proof, if that's what you're asking. But if you're taking a survey, yeah. Joanne and her cousin killed her husband. Everybody knows it. Nobody can prove it."

"Her cousin Luca?"

"Yeah, that one."

"What do you know about Luca?"

"I know what everyone knows. I know to stay away from him."

"Because he's violent?"

"Because he's professionally violent. The Amatos and the Di Stefanos are connected to Big John Giacomo. Luca is their muscle."

The name Giacomo didn't mean much to me, but I assumed he was up to no good. It could be drugs, gambling, prostitution, extortion, loan sharking. All sorts of charming things.

"Luca has a trucking company, you know what it's called?"

She knew, I could see it in her face, but she shrugged anyway. After a moment, she said, "Hold on." She disappeared, then was back with a thick Yellow Pages.

I took it from her and set it on top of the glass case. As I flipped through, I realized I wasn't even sure what it meant to have a trucking company. Was that shipping or moving? Or was it both? And once I figured that out, how would I know which one belonged to...

Oh, wow. That turned out not to be hard. I went to TRUCKING first and halfway down the list, I found LUCA'S LIFTERS. I guess that meant he provided in-town moving services. I wrote down the address: 12 Mile Road. It didn't sound too hard to find since I'd already been on 10 Mile Road. It must be a few blocks north of that.

I said thank you to the woman who's name I hadn't learned—probably because she'd rather I didn't know it—and left the bakery with my biscotti. I took one out and crunched on it as I drove north. Dropping crumbs on the front seat, I passed 7 Mile Road, 8, 9... eventually I got to 12 Mile Road. I made a wrong turn, then doubled back until I found the street address I was looking for.

It looked wrong. I was expecting something like a parking lot full of trucks with a small building where an office was housed. What I found was two office buildings, each two-stories tall and brick—looking a lot like Cass's high school. There was a parking lot running around the buildings on all sides.

I double-checked the address. It was the right one. I drove around the buildings checking the parking lot for moving vans. I didn't see any. The closest I came was a gray Chevy Suburban with tinted windows and a white van sitting next to each other, not too far from the entrance to the building on the west side.

I parked, shut the car off and went inside. I took a biscotti with me and ate it while staring at a directory made with moveable plastic letters. Luca's Lifting was on the second floor in room 207. I thought about taking the stairs. It was only one floor. But instead I went to the elevator and pressed the UP button.

It didn't take long for the elevator to arrive. I tried to sort out what I'd be saying to whoever was in Luca's office. I need to hire a mover—that part was simple. But why didn't I just call? I was in the neighborhood and decided to stop by? I was a building inspector? I'm looking for a different Luca?

I hadn't decided, and I was already walking down the hallway to the office. Some of the doors I passed had plaques that gave the business' name but none of the offices seemed very active. The floor was particularly quiet.

When I reached 207, I hesitated before knocking. I leaned close and pressed my ear up against the door. There was nothing to hear. I stepped back and knocked on the door. Waited. Nothing happened. I knocked again. Waited again. Nothing. No one worked there.

CHAPTER FIFTEEN

B y the time I found The Clock Diner a second time it was close to noon. I was hungry and I had an idea I wanted to pursue. I came back to The Clock Diner since it hadn't been half bad and I kind of remembered where it was. I was able to snag the very last booth next to the bathroom and the pay phone. I ordered coffee, since I hadn't had enough, and the lumberjack breakfast with eggs over easy and bacon. I loved places that served breakfast all day. When the rather sullen waitress walked away, I got up to use the pay phone.

Using the phone book that was attached to the pay phone, I found the number for Luca's Lifters and dialed it. I wasn't expecting an answer, so I wasn't surprised when an answering machine picked up. I was a little surprised when Joanne told me no one was available to take my call and I should call back during regular business hours. I *was* calling during regular business hours, but you can't exactly argue with a machine.

The phone call did tell me one thing: The whole operation was fake. Luca hadn't even bothered to hire a fake receptionist to answer the phone and tell people they were too busy to do their move. They probably just never called anyone back.

I stood there a moment, thinking about how he worked it. There had to be trucks somewhere, possibly not even operational, and he had to spend some time filling out invoices and then "paying" them in cash. That would be how he was laundering the money he got from whatever small piece of Big John's business belonged to him.

Using my calling card, I placed another call. It was about nine-fifteen in California.

"Freedom Agenda," Karen said when she answered.

"It's Dom."

"I'll get Lydia."

"Actually—"

"Actually, you have a favor to ask."

"I do."

With a well-practiced sigh, she said, "Go ahead."

"I need to find a small-time thug connected to the Detroit Partnership who died sometime after 1982."

"What's his name?"

"That's the part I need."

"You know that's not how a Boolean search works?"

I didn't completely know what that meant, but I got the gist. "Do you think you can do it in the next hour? I don't have my mobile phone with me. I'm at a diner."

That was met by a very chilly silence. I went ahead and gave her the number on the pay phone.

"This isn't connected to one of our cases, is it?"

"No."

"I'll have to ask Lydia."

"Is she there?"

"Hold on."

A few moments later, Lydia picked up. "What happened to you?"

"I have some things to take care of."

"Who was that kid?"

"Uh... well, in a way he's my son."

"In a way?"

"A nonbiological way. His name is Cassidy Reilly."

"Oh. Oh my God! Where are you?"

"Detroit."

"How long will you be there?"

"Maybe I'll come home tonight. It depends."

"Do you need anything from me?"

"Actually, I need Karen to—"

"She's already on it. Though it doesn't make much sense."

My breakfast/lunch arrived and I was about to say good-bye when I remembered something. "Hey, do you know what alprazolam is?"

"Xanax. My doctor gave me some after the shooting. It's for anxiety."

A few months before, when I'd shot a man in the lobby of our offices Lydia had taken the blame. I could see how that might make her anxious. Joanne on the other hand was one of the least anxious people I've ever met. She was either taking the drugs recreationally or they were working very well. I thanked her and said good-bye. Then I sat down in the booth and dug into my breakfast. It was perfect.

Long after I'd finished breakfast, around my fourth cup of coffee, the pay phone rang. I got up and answered. Not bothering with hello, Karen said, "Vito Giancarlo. Twenty-eight at the time of his death in 1986. A couple years before, he was contracted to put a bomb in this guy's car. It didn't go off so he got caught. He turned on his boss, a guy named Ferretti. Which resulted in his getting stuck with a shiv in Marquette prison."

"Perfect."

"You owe me."

"I know. I won't forget."

After I hung up, I paid my bill, adding a large tip for sitting at the table for so long. Then went out to the car and drove to Top Dog Collections. When I walked in, Claudia was sitting at the desk. She had earphones in her ears listening to a Discman as she typed. From the sound leaking out I think it was Luther Vandross. As soon as she saw me, her eyes widened and she shook her head a little.

Pulling out one of the earphones, she said, "Good afternoon, how can I help you, sir?"

"I'm here to see Ms. Di Stefano."

Claudia stood, smoothed her skirt, which had wrinkled around the hips, and led me over to Joanne's office. "Gentleman here to see you," she said before getting out of my way.

Joanne took one look at me, and said, "Come in and shut the door." As soon as I had, she hissed, "What the fuck are you doing here?"

The office was just as it had been the day before, except there was an expensive purse on the credenza and the purple leather coat on a coatrack. She hadn't lied when she said she wanted to wear it more often. Probably one of the few truthful things she'd said to me.

I sat down casually. "So this is the deal I have with your son. If I find out who killed his dad then I get to keep using his identity."

"Why would he make a deal like that?"

"He says he's going to kill that person when I find them."

After a moment of silence, she said, "That doesn't work for me."

"No, I don't imagine it would."

And that was as close as we came to acknowledging the fact that she'd killed her husband. Normally, I'd be a lot more interested in seeing a killer get what they deserve, particularly in a situation like this one where I couldn't see that the real Dom Reilly deserved what he got. The problem was, I didn't want to see Cass in prison for killing his mother. Or anyone else for that matter.

"I have a solution. I did some research and there was a guy named Vito Giancarlo who admitted to placing a bomb in someone's car around 1984. He flipped on the people who ordered the hit. He wasn't in prison long before he got knifed with a sharpened toothbrush. So he's dead."

"I might have heard something about that. Vito was a friend of a friend. So what?"

"Last night you said someone told you Dominick was killed accidentally but you wouldn't say by who. Tell the kid you made a couple of calls and found out it was Vito. That Vito killed his dad. And that'll be the end of it."

"And you get to go home and keep being Dominick Reilly."

"Exactly."

"What do I get out of it?"

"Uh... your son doesn't murder you and you stay out of prison. That should be enough."

"Except it's not." She pushed away from the desk and crossed her legs, then continued, "Cass tells me you went to see Suzie Reilly. That house belonged to her parents. They left it to Suzie *and* Dominick. That means half the house belongs to you; technically. I want you to sign it over to me."

"Suzie knows I'm not her brother."

"And you're leaving town and never coming back. We'll do it all via the mail."

"Still, I don't think I can stand up to that level of scrutiny. You know how fragile a fake identity can be."

"You don't need to worry about it. Tony will handle the details."

"Tony?"

"Short for Anton. Mr. Cray. My boss."

There was no way I was going to go along with this. For one thing, it was mean. For another, I didn't think it would work.

"I keep hearing it was your cousin Luca who killed your husband. And that you asked him to."

"Who says that? I'll kill them!"

"You might want to remove murder from your repertoire. It's not working out well."

There was a tapping on the door, then it opened. Mr. Cray stepped in. He was in his late fifties, small and wiry with hard black eyes and a full head of white hair. He'd probably been very handsome when he was younger. Now he was distinguished.

"Is everything all right, Joanne?"

"Everything's fine, Tony. Thanks for checking in."

He didn't move. Instead, he waited for me to say something. "I'm a friend of Joanne's son."

I don't think he liked that much.

"I'll explain later," Joanne told him. In other words, she needed some time to make up a lie.

"If you need me, I'm right next door."

"You're a doll."

Reluctantly, he shut the door. As soon as it was closed, Joanne said, "We should talk about getting a divorce."

"Actually I'm surprised you didn't try to have me declared dead."

"I had my reasons."

Which might have to do with the credit cards she took out in my name. Or rather Dominick's name.

"I ran your credit this morning. You have assets."

"Don't even think it."

I saw red for a moment but then calmed. I'd seen *her* assets. Most of my assets were in Ronnie's name. Only the co-op had my name on it—well, half of it. All told, my assets amounted to around fifty thousand dollars. As I recalled, her assets were at least double that.

"And of course there's thirteen years of child support," she added.

"I'll get a DNA test. Prove he's not my kid."

"Fine. Just your assets then."

"You have assets, too. Which I would be just as entitled to. In fact you have more assets than I do. So you'd owe me money. Except..." I left a deliberately long pause. "...your assets stem from fraud or embezzlement, I'm not sure which exactly. It would be a terrible thing if that came out during a divorce."

Her face fell for a moment but then quickly recovered. She got up, walked a couple of steps to a credenza and turned a radio on to a classical station. She looked unnerved. She'd had no idea I knew all that. She was stalling to catch her balance.

"Don't forget I can expose you."

"I haven't forgotten. How about we skip mutually assured destruction and each keep what we have?"

Unhappily, she agreed. I didn't believe her for a moment.

"You're still young," I pointed out. "I'm sure you can find a man with more assets than I have. Provided they don't find out who you really are."

A light went off behind her eyes. She'd heard exactly what I wanted her to hear. If she fucked with me, I'd fuck with her. And not just now. Always. I was taking a risk and I knew it.

"Well, I guess we're just going to have to be friends."

"Or something like it."

We went over the plan one more time. She'd reluctantly tell Cass that she'd found out Vito Giancarlo killed his father. She'd refuse to say who gave her this information for safety reasons. I was hoping he'd buy it.

After I left, I drove around until I saw a pay phone on the side of a 7-Eleven—a different one, not my home away from home. I pulled in, got out my calling card, and then sat in the car for a good ten minutes.

Joanne Di Stefano was a piece of work. I didn't have any reason to think she'd keep her end of any bargain. Yeah, I thought she'd go along with the story I wanted to tell Cass about Vito Giancarlo. It fit her purposes. For now. But who knew about next month or next year or the year after that.

I got out of the car and called Ronnie on his cellular.

"Hello."

"It's me."

"You haven't called in two days."

"I wanted to wait until I knew when I'd be coming home."

"No. You call me every day. I don't care if you have nothing to say. I just need to hear your voice."

"I'm coming home. Maybe later tonight. Probably not until tomorrow."

"You mean home as in Long Beach. You *are* home right now, aren't you?"

It took a moment for the penny to drop. "Oh. You mean Detroit. It's not my home anymore."

"I called the credit card company. I've been following you all along."

"I've spent a lot of money. I'm sorry, I'll make it up to you."

"You don't have to do that. Financially, you've more than held up your end. I don't begrudge you the money."

"But..."

"I hate not knowing where you are. And I hate sleeping alone. The silence is terrible."

The 'silence' was a reference to my snoring, which, given the number of times I'd had my nose broken, was quite impressive.

"Where are you?" he asked.

"Detroit. We established that."

"I mean exactly. I hear traffic. It sounds like you're outside."

"I'm on a pay phone in front of a 7-Eleven."

"That's romantic."

"Not really."

"Don't you remember? The night we met we sat in your car outside a 7-Eleven having coffee and donuts. It was like three or four in the morning."

"I do remember. Of course, I remember. We got chased off. Right after I told you I'd killed a man."

"See. I told it was romantic. Have you killed anyone since you got to Detroit?"

"No. I've been tempted though."

"How is the kid? He's not gay is he?"

"No. He has a Pavlovian response to attractive young women."

"Well, that's a relief."

"Where are you?" I asked.

"In my car, waiting for clients. They're late. The house is one point two million though, so if they buy it I'll forgive them."

I did some quick math and his commission on that price would be close to forty thousand dollars, which might be another reason he wasn't too concerned about my spending.

CHAPTER SIXTEEN

September 16, 1996
Monday afternoon

While I was waiting for Cass to come out of the high school, something tumbled for me. There was no computer on Joanne's desk in her den. The computer was upstairs on Cass's desk next to a laser printer. A laser printer. A kid like Cass didn't need a laser printer. Not to mention they were expensive. Ronnie was angling for one for Christmas. Four hundred dollars.

Joanne needed a laser printer though, to write her letters from Top Dawg. But then I doubted very much she went into Cass's disgusting room to write the letters, so she'd have had her son do them.

Everything seemed to be in his name. She'd been setting him up. I was sure she used his age to justify it to herself. He'd begun working at Top Dog when he was fifteen. It made sense to blame him. Worst case scenario he'd go to juvie—and she'd go nowhere.

Cass was one of the last students to come out of the building. He slunk over to the car and got in.

"What took so long?"

He shrugged. I waited. Then he said, "Teacher kept me after class. She said I'm smart and if I tried harder I could get good grades. Bitch."

"Oh yeah, that is bitchy." I'd pegged him on the plane, I was a little proud of myself. I asked, "So why not try harder?"

"What for?"

"Yeah, I guess you're right. It would be a shame if you did well in life."

He gave me a disdainful glance. "Nobody cares about your grades in high school. They just care if you got the diploma."

"I think there's more to it than that."

"Just drive, okay?"

Before we got to his house, he asked what I'd done that day. I told him about my trip to the bakery and checking out Luca's Lifts. Of course, I left out my trip to see his mother. But I did start to lay the groundwork for my plan.

"We need to convince your mother to tell us who told her your father was beaten to death by mistake and see if that person can tell us who actually killed him. Once we find out, I'm going home."

I said the last very firmly, wanting to get him used to the idea I was leaving. I parked the car in front of his house. We got out and went inside. He went immediately to the kitchen, pulled open the drawer with take-out menus, and began going through them.

"Do you have homework?"

"Yeah, like that's what's important." He'd picked out three of the menus. "On Mondays we have Chinese."

Standing behind him, I noticed that each of the menus had dates written on top. They were spreading things out. Probably because they were using fraudulent credit cards and didn't want to charge too much in one spot.

He looked at the clock; it was 3:50. He went over to the wall phone and dialed the number for a place called Dragon House.

"Yeah, I want to order for pick-up. I want a lemon chicken with extra white rice, shrimp fried rice, and two egg rolls." He listened. "Forty-five minutes? Great. And make sure it's hot. The name is..." He reached into his jeans and pulled out a card and read it. "Blansky. Brian Blansky."

After he hung up, he said, "My mom likes to eat at five-fifteen sharp. You need to be gone. I'll drop you at Motel 6."

"I'd like to have a conversation with your mother."

"I don't think she wants to talk to you."

"Okay. Then I'll go home. Take me to the airport."

"You're not going anywhere until we know who killed my dad."

"If that's the deal then you need to actually let me find out for you. I need to talk to your mother."

There was struggle on his face. He really didn't want to displease her, but there was no other way to get to the truth. Or at least there wasn't the way I was presenting it.

"Yeah, okay, whatever."

"Call back and add a beef and broccoli to your order. I think I deserve dinner."

"Jesus Christ," he said, but he did it.

Driving to Dragon House, I kept thinking if my plan worked I would be leaving in a few hours and never have to see this kid again. That wasn't a bad thing. I wouldn't mind never seeing him again.

I mean, I didn't hate the kid. As kidnappers go, he wasn't bad. I did feel sorry for him, though. With Joanne for a mother he didn't have a chance. He'd mentioned that he had to get out of her house when he graduated high school. That meant he had about eight months, maybe nine. It was hard to see how he was going to manage on his own. It seemed the only things he was good at were credit card fraud and coercion. He'd end up in prison before he was twenty-one.

"You should think about college. I bet your Aunt Suzie would help you figure that out. They have dorms. You'd have some place to live for four years."

"I'll be fine."

"I didn't say you wouldn't be. But maybe there's something better than just fine. That's all I'm saying."

When we got to Dragon House he told me to stay in the car. Probably because he was sick of listening to me. I sat there staring at the red lacquered door. I knew it was entirely possible Joanne wasn't going to keep her word. Hell, it was *likely* she wouldn't. So what was she going to do?

She'd run a credit check on me and wanted to get her hands on my rather scant assets. Would she really have me killed for fifty thousand dollars? I was ninety-nine percent sure she'd killed her husband, so yeah, why wouldn't she?

And this time she'd have to have a body. Mine. She'd just need to make sure that neither my fingerprints or DNA were checked. They had my fingerprints in Chicago. I was sure of that. But I didn't know what organizations they'd been shared with. I'd heard talk about some kind of national computerized database but didn't know if that had happened yet. Joanne wouldn't know either.

She'd be hoping the police just took her word for it when she identified my body... Except, at some point Suzie was going to want to see her brother's body. And that would be a problem. A big problem. The whole reason to kill me was so she could say I was her husband and get my stuff. If she thought it through she'd know it was bad idea. The question was... would she think it through?

On the other hand, maybe it was better not to have a body. If she called her cousin and had me put at the bottom of Lake Erie with the first Dom Reilly she'd only have to wait five years or so to have him (or me) declared dead. At that point she could try to attach my half of the co-op, which by then will be a condo and worth substantially more. That was a better plan. Not that I intended to explain that to her.

The kid came back with a big bag that he put in the back seat. As we pulled out of the parking lot to head home, I asked, "Do you have take-out every night?"

"Monday is Chinese, Tuesday is Mexican, Wednesday is Pizza, Thursday is Greek, Friday night my mom goes out to dinner. On Sundays we have Italian. Lasagna or Manicotti."

"Italian from a restaurant?"

"Of course from a restaurant. Pretty girls don't have to cook."

"That's what your mom says?"

"Everyone knows that."

I decided that wasn't a point I wanted to argue. After a bit, I said, "It's hard being a kid, isn't it?"

"What's that supposed to mean?"

"I remember when I was a teenager everyone said I had it easy. But I didn't really. In a lot of ways life gets easier when you get older." And harder, too. But I wasn't going to tell him that. He'd learn it on his own.

"I'm fine. I don't know what you're talking about."

Except, of course, he did. If his life was easy he wouldn't be looking for his father. Or willing to blackmail someone into finding out what happened to him. If his life was easy he'd be more focused on learning. If his life was easy he might think college was possible.

But his life wasn't easy and the closer we got to his house the edgier he got. I finally asked, "What's going on with you? You seem really nervous."

"We're running late. She hates when she gets home and dinner's not there."

What I wanted to say was 'Wow, what a bitch,' but I went with, "I'm sure she'll be okay about it."

"You don't know her."

"I'll be there. I'll get her to calm down."

That got a chuckle out of him. "Good luck with that."

And then we pulled up to the house. He parked on the street. Yeah, I was right. He wasn't allowed to park in the driveway I had to pick up the pace to keep up with him. He rushed through the front door and into the kitchen. As he did, he called out, "Mom. We're here. We've got dinner. And it's hot!"

Silence.

Cass set the bag down on the kitchen counter, then continued over to the door to the garage. He opened and stuck his head inside. Then he backed out.

"Her car's not there."

"I guess you lucked out."

"No, it's weird. She never stays late."

I glanced at the clock on the microwave. It was 5:35. "It takes fifteen minutes to drive home?"

"Twenty. But she always leaves five minutes early. Mr. Cray usually leaves at four."

"Must be nice."

"They work hard," he said, defensively.

"Maybe you should call the office, just in case."

He walked over to the wall phone and dialed. The phone still had a rotary dial instead of buttons. I guessed that it was here when they bought the house and Joanne didn't want to pay to replace it.

Cass turned around and looked at me, saying, "No one's answering." He hung up and said, "We should go to Top Dog. Maybe her car broke down."

"It looked like it's just a couple of years old. Why would it breakdown?"

"I don't know. Maybe it's a lemon."

"Then why hasn't she called you? She'd call you if her car broke down, wouldn't she?"

He walked back through the house to Joanne's office. I followed him. He was staring at the answering machine.

"There aren't any messages. We should go."

"Put the dinner in the oven so it doesn't cool off too fast."

He heard me, but he didn't pay any attention. I followed him outside and we got into the Belvedere.

"What if she comes home while we're gone?" I asked.

"I don't know. It's all kind of weird. She's never late. Never. She's a good mom."

Not the time to disagree with that.

"We'll find her," I said, trying to sound reassuring. I had no idea what was going on.

It didn't take us twenty minutes to get back to Top Dog. He drove at least fifteen miles over the speed limit and the car had a very powerful engine.

As we approached the parking lot, I could see that there were six black-and-white patrol cars. There were a lot of people, mostly police officers standing around. At the center of it all I could see glimpses of a bronze car. A bronze Eldorado. On the pavement next to the car, a sliver of purple that had to be Joanne.

"Don't turn in," I said, as firmly as I could. "Keep driving."

"What? No. Why?"

"Do what I fucking tell you."

Cass stared at me. Shocked. Then we passed the parking lot. "What's happening? Something's happening."

"Go around the corner and pull over."

"Why? We should go back. I'm going to turn around."

But he didn't, he pulled over like I told him.

"I'm going to drive."

"It's my car. We need to go back. Something's hap—" And then it seemed to flood him. "That was my mom, wasn't it?"

"Yeah. It was your mom."

"We have to go back."

"It's not going to help. She was lying on the ground. No one was helping her. There was no ambulance."

"Then it's on its way!"

"You said your mom was punctual. Whatever happened, happened almost an hour ago."

He started to gasp. I undid his safety belt and pulled him across the bench seat. I pulled him over me as I slid toward the driver's seat. It would have been absurdly funny if the kid wasn't starting to sob and my shoulder didn't scream bloody murder. Well, that might be a poor choice of words.

My mind was racing, skipping around, jumping at different ideas. There were a few things I was sure of.

"Okay. You need to calm down," I told Cass. "There are a few things we need to do, and then you can go ahead and lose your shit."

He looked at me in horror. "What?"

"Technically, I'm Dom Reilly. I just showed up out of nowhere and now my wife is dead. That makes me the prime suspect. Meanwhile, you've been embezzling from your mother's place of employ—"

"It wasn't me. It was—"

"Your name is on everything. The police will tell themselves a story that she found out and you killed her over it. That makes you prime suspect number two."

I pulled out into the street and began driving back to his house. I kept talking. "We don't have much time. The police are going to show up within an hour to do the notification. That's when you want to turn on the waterworks."

"Fuck you."

"We have to get the file with all those credit cards and anything else that refers to Top Dawg – D-A-W-G. We also need to get the shoe box full of cash out of your mother's closet."

"How do you—you weren't supposed to go in there."

"You need to be glad I did. Is there anything I missed?"

"I don't know."

"You'd better know, unless you want to go to prison."

"I didn't do anything."

"I'm not a DA, but you're definitely guilty of credit card fraud. A lot of credit card fraud. But that's not the point. Is there anything else suspicious in the house?"

"There's a gun."

"Where is it?"

"Under my bed."

"Where did it come from?"

"Luca gave it to my mother to hide."

"Which means it was probably used in a crime. Or at the very least it's stolen and can't be traced back to Luca. Either way you shouldn't have it."

"You're acting like the police are going to search the house. I won't let them do that."

"And if you don't you move up the suspect list."

"I have an alibi. I was with you."

"And I can't be anywhere near this."

"That's your problem."

"No, Cass... it's your problem."

And then I parked in the driveway. Not bothering with the steering wheel lock, I jumped out of the car and ran to the house. Cass came up behind me and unlocked the front door.

Inside, I rushed to the den and grabbed the accordion folder from the desk and then went upstairs for the shoebox from Joanne's closet. Meanwhile, Cass got the gun from under his bed. It took some time so either he had another burst of emotion or it was buried under there pretty deep. It was in a Macy's bag. I looked inside, the gun was a 9MM Ruger, scratched up and badly in need of a cleaning. It looked like it had been buried.

"Where's the nearest pay phone. I need to call a cab."

"You can call from here."

"Not if they check your phone records."

"Shit."

"Yeah, don't call anyone except your Aunt Suzie. Speaking of which, where will I find a pay phone? Is there a gas station nearby?"

"You probably want to go to the 7-Eleven right off 10 Mile Road."

I'd already been there. It wasn't exactly close. As I walked out the slider into the backyard, he asked, "You're coming back aren't you?"

"Tomorrow," I said, and I had a sick feeling I meant it.

CHAPTER SEVENTEEN

September 16, 1996
Monday evening

There used to be this thing called flophouses. At some point, corporate America decided that was a business they wanted to be in. Later that night I moved out of Motel 6 and moved into a hotel that was even cheaper and significantly more disgusting. This time, I registered as Charles Henderson and let him pay my bill.

It had taken until sunset to get to the 7-Eleven and call a cab to take me to the nearest car rental place. Hertz turned out to be around the corner, so to make it worthwhile for the cabbie I had him take me to their office in Livonia. I knew I wouldn't be renting the car as Dom Reilly, but still it might be better if Charles Henderson wasn't too close at hand. Just in case.

When I got to Hertz I asked for a Crown Vic—I might as well look like a cop—but they didn't have any. The clerk threatened me with an Aspire, which was more like a go-cart than a car. I finally got him to offer me a black Escort. Four doors. Not ideal, but it would do.

Before I switched hotels I dropped in at a Kinkos. They had a FedEx desk. I bought a large envelope, slipped my driver's license, phone card and credit cards inside, addressed it to myself in Long Beach and sent it overnight. I was temporarily Charles Henderson.

I checked out of Motel Six, then drove down the street to my new flophouse—er, motel. The new clerk didn't even ask for my temporary license. Henderson's credit card was enough to capture his interest. There were a couple of people in the lobby who looked like they were waiting for a ride to the methadone clinic. And as soon as I had that thought I realized it was probably offensive to drug addicts everywhere.

In the room, every single outlet was broken, the grout around the bathtub was crumbling, the sheets had been washed so many times the only thing holding them together was residual grime, the TV didn't work, the fixtures in the bathroom were so dirty they needed to be replaced. But, hey, for the moment it was home.

It wasn't a long moment. After I choked down the rest of my Tylenol with water from the bathroom sink, I decided to go back out. But not until I debated whether to leave the Macy's bag full of credit cards, cash and a gun in the room. The only thing keeping me from being robbed was an electronic lock opened by a plastic card. I took the bag with me.

Driving around, I made a mental list. I needed something to eat. None of that Chinese food had come my way. I needed some bottled water—I'd probably already gotten dysentery from the pipes at the corporate flophouse. I found a place called Meijer, which was huge, an aircraft hangar for food. I bought a loaf of bread, some deli meat, a small bottle of mayonnaise, a six pack of root beer, some bottled water, a large bottle of Tylenol, and a package of plastic silverware. At the last minute I threw some bran muffins in the cart for breakfast. They had a men's section, so I bought another pack of underwear—I'd gotten separated from the last pack, some socks, T-shirts and a shirt with a collar. I had the feeling I was going to need it.

I'd take a couple hundred out of the shoebox, which was now in the trunk of the Escort, and paid with that. I had no idea when Charles Henderson's card would tap out and I didn't want to find out the hard way. Of course, I had a half dozen more credit cards, but I didn't feel great about using them. Yeah, the cash was also probably ill-gotten, but at least it didn't come with names attached.

On the way home from Meijer I drove by the Top Dog Collection offices. The police cars were gone except for one beige Crown Vic, as was

Joanne's body. A flatbed truck was pulling the Eldorado onto it's flatbed. There was yellow crime tape attached to sticks stuck into cement blocks surrounding the area. A White guy and a Black woman in suits were carefully walking the area with flashlights. That told me something I'd already guessed: Joanne had been shot. They were looking for bullet casings. I kept driving, doing my best not to look conspicuous.

The clock on the dashboard said it was ten after eleven. I decided to take a drive by Cass's house. *Was* it Cass's house now? I remember the mortgage was over two grand a month. It might not be his house for long. Not unless Joanne had life insurance and somehow I found that unlikely. Obviously, I'd be giving him back his mother's cash and he'd find his way to the Top Dawg accounts. But I doubted at seventeen he'd be making wise financial decisions. Would he make it through a year there? Two?

When I turned onto their street, I immediately saw there were a lot of cars parked nearby. Ten maybe. I slowed to get a good look at them. The old Belvedere was in the driveway where I'd parked it. Squeezed behind it was a brown Plymouth Voyager with a Clinton/Gore bumper sticker; that had to be Suzie Reilly. She'd mentioned the Voyager when we met. Also on the street were two black Cadillacs, both Sedan DeVilles and a blue Corvette with a big white strip down the center. As I continued down the street, a Chevy Suburban with blacked out windows and a white van drove by me—the same two vehicles I'd seen sitting outside Luca's office building. I slowed and watched as they continued past the house and down the street.

I was curious so I circled the block. After walking through the neighborhood I was familiar with the streets. The houses were all similar to Joanne's. The lots weren't especially large, with the houses themselves taking up most of the space. People here didn't bother much with fences. I'd been able to walk through several yards on my way to the 7-Eleven.

And then, there was the Suburban and the van again. We passed each other. I kept my head turned in the other direction, as though I was looking for something. At the end of the block, I put the blinker on to go left and then switched to the right. I turned right and drove away. Hopefully, they bought me as simply being lost and not someone scoping out the same property they were looking at.

By the time I got back to the flophouse, I was sure I knew who was in the Suburban. Feds. Luca was being watched by some branch of the

Federal government. Probably the FBI. Though it could also be ATF or DEA.

I doubted it was the state of Michigan, though. The white van had to hold the kind of microphones and recording equipment you can aim at a building and hear what people are saying inside. That was expensive and required some expertise. Honestly, I didn't know much about that kind of work except that was illegal for private investigators and not a great idea without a warrant. But the Feds never seemed to have much trouble getting warrants.

Back at the corporate flophouse, I took a shower which didn't make me feel clean. Then I got into the bed and stared at the ceiling for what seemed like hours. I must have slept, because I woke up thinking about a man I'd loved, Bert Harker. The anniversary of his death was coming up. The twenty-eighth. It would be fourteen years. Not for the first time, I found myself wondering what might have happened if he hadn't been murdered, if he hadn't been dying of AIDS, if he hadn't sacrificed himself. Would we have stayed together? Would we still be together? Would it have been easier to lose him if our relationship had died a natural death?

He wasn't the first man I'd loved, or even the first I'd lost. But he was the hardest loss. I wondered for a moment if that was why I was fighting so hard to keep my life together. Because I knew what loss was. Then I had to laugh at myself. These were the kinds of things you should never think about early in the morning in a disgusting hotel. I got out of bed and began my day, knowing it was going to be a long one.

I drove back to Livonia and got breakfast in an old-style diner called Two Brothers. It hadn't been redecorated in three decades, which suited me just fine. I sat at the counter, and a waitress—who looked like she'd been working there since the place opened—brought over a coffee pot, flipped over the thick mug in front of me, and filled it all without offering me a menu.

"You want the special?"

I had no idea what it was, but decided to go with it. "Yeah, sure."

"How do you want your eggs?"

"Over easy."

"Bacon or sausage?"

"Bacon."

A TV sat on a giant microwave. The *Today* show was playing, though the reception was poor. It wasn't busy, so I asked, "You mind turning that up a little?"

She obviously minded but did it anyway. Katie Couric was interviewing Bette Midler about a movie she had coming out, *First Wives Club*. Ronnie was excited about it. He loved Bette Midler. I liked her music, but I wasn't always sure about her as an actress. Instead of talking about the movie, Katie was asking about Bette's marriage to a German guy.

The coffee was bad in just the right way: too strong; which I liked. Breakfast came quickly. French toast, hash browns, the eggs and bacon. Also bad but greasy enough to make up for it. I was pouring syrup on the toast when the local news came on. It was almost seven-thirty.

The news anchor, in heavy makeup and hairspray, began: "A local woman was gunned down in what police are calling a failed carjacking. Joanne Di Stefano was killed outside her place of employ. At this time, there are no suspects. Our hearts go out to her family. In other news..."

'A failed carjacking'? What did that mean? Did they have security footage from the building? And if so, what did it show? The door to the Eldorado was open when we drove by. That suggests she was shot while trying to get into the car. Was her purse stolen? And why do they think the killer didn't take the car?

Right away, I doubted it was carjacking. Cass and I had been going around asking questions for three days about a thirteen-year-old disappearance/murder. We'd stirred something up. It just made sense. Of course, the police had no idea what I'd been up to. At least, not yet.

On the TV, Matt Lauer was talking about Bob Dole's ideas about getting tough on crime. An always popular issue to run on, but not one that ever gets solved. Clinton got the backing of the biggest police officers union, as if to counter the first story. And a new study showed that most people on welfare were White, lived in rural areas, and stayed on the program for less than a year. I was surprised that even got reported. It wasn't what people wanted to hear and my guess was it would be forgotten pretty quickly. I paid my check and left. The TV was turned down before I got to the door.

Then I drove back to Hertz. I was probably being paranoid, but the Feds had seen the Escort. It looked a bit too much like a rental to be inconspicuous. That was the irony of inconspicuous vehicles. If you knew what to look for, they weren't inconspicuous at all. They had a dark blue Thunderbird so I took it. I'd appreciate the extra room, at least.

When I left Hertz, I went right to the K-Mart Cass had taken me to. I had a feeling they'd have what I wanted in sporting goods. I needed a kit to clean the gun Cass had given me and some ammo. It was a bad idea to clean the gun and buy ammo. But here's the thing: Guns are always a bad idea until they're not. And then, at least half the time, they're still a bad idea. Sometimes, though, bad ideas are all you have.

While I was there I picked up a hunting jacket with big pockets—the puffer vest I'd purchased just three days before was still in Cass's junk room with some unused underwear and an orange sweatshirt. That didn't matter, though, its pockets weren't big enough. The jacket I bought was military green with zippered ten-inch pockets. I'd have a way to carry my bad idea around with me.

I stood still in the middle of the store and tried to think if I needed anything else. This was the third time I'd been in one of these giant stores in as many days. That wasn't great.

On the way out I picked up a bottle of cologne, Aramis. The possibility of my ending up dead on this trip had been increasing. I thought I'd like to smell good for my autopsy.

CHAPTER EIGHTEEN

September 17, 1996
Tuesday morning

I was back at the corporate flophouse by ten-thirty. I cleaned the Ruger as best I could, then loaded it. I had no idea if it would fire. Hopefully, I'd never have to find out. I put on the shirt with a collar I'd bought, dabbed on some Aramis, pulled the tags off my new jacket and put it on. The gun fit nicely in the pocket.

Then I drove back to Top Dog. Except for a few scraps here and there, the crime scene tape was gone, but they'd left the cement blocks. There was a janitor with a bucket and a mop working on the spot where Joanne's body had been.

I drove around the building looking for two thing: first, a silver BMW and second, security cameras. I didn't see any BMWs. I did see security cameras at the front entrance, which would include the front parking lot where Joanne was killed, the back entrance, and one side, the west side. I made a second ring around the building and parked near the back entrance.

On the first floor, like the second, a long hallway ran from one end of the building to another. I walked to the front. That's where the security desk was. It looked just the same as it had on Sunday. There was clipboard for signing in but no security officer. That seemed odd. Especially, the day after a shooting.

I stepped behind the desk, which was custom-made. There was a cheap monitor hidden beneath the shelf where the clipboard sat. The screen was split into three: One angle showed the front parking lot—the janitor was still out there with his mop; another showed the west parking lot.

There was something odd about the desk and it took a moment to figure out what it was. Then it hit me like cold water to the face. There was nothing personal on the desk. No photographs of kids, no cute pencil erasers, no mints, no take-out menus, no souvenir coffee cups. Nothing. The desk was there to give the appearance of security—and nothing else.

I went up to the second floor and walked down to the Top Dog offices. I turned the knob and the door opened. Claudia was sitting at her desk, Discman plugged into her ears. Taking the earphones out, she said, "My, my, my... look who's back."

"Hello Claudia. It's awful about Joanne, isn't it?"

"I guess," she said. And that seemed to sum up their relationship.

"I was wondering... is there ever a security guard downstairs?"

"I've never seen one."

"Can you tell me what you've heard about what happened?"

"What have I heard?" She snorted. "Well, I've heard that some *Black* kid came up from the city and tried to steal a White lady's car but couldn't even manage to do that right. That's what I've heard. That's what people say to my black face."

"And by people you mean the police?"

"I don't know that people is the best way to describe the police, but yeah... that's who I mean."

"What do you think happened?"

"Isn't it obvious? Her whole family's in the Mafia. One of them decided to whack her."

She was right. That was more likely than some random kid from the city. I doubted it was the whole story. I also doubted the police would do much more than look for a Black kid in the wrong neighborhood.

"Did anyone actually see what happened?"

"Not that I've heard. There's a lot of empty offices in this building."

"Did you leave before or after Joanne?"

"I work ten to seven. Those last two hours I make calls."

I didn't ask whether she made them for Tog Dog or herself.

"I went out when I heard the sirens. Everybody was out there. It was like a fire drill."

"When did Mr. Cray leave?"

"Right after Joanne."

Something bothered me about that, but I forged ahead. "Did he see what happened?"

"I don't think so. He called to tell me he wasn't coming in. He's kind of in shock, I think. Could barely talk about it. Anyway, he parks in the back. His car is crazy expensive. He was always telling Joanne she shouldn't park in front."

"Wait, did he always leave *after* Joanne?"

"He usually left at four, sometimes three-thirty."

"Did he say why he was leaving late?"

"He didn't have to. He dumped a stack of filings on my desk. Said he wanted them in the mail first thing."

"Was that unusual?"

"No. He's like that. Most of the time he's not that interested in what we're doing, then he runs around like chicken with its head cut off... fits and starts, fits and starts."

"Do you know who found the body?"

"Some lady down the hall. Re-insurance, I think. What do you think of that? An insurance company has to have insurance. What's the world coming to? Pretty soon we'll all be doing nothing but insuring each other."

"Did you talk to her?"

"No. Everybody was treating her like she was some kind of movie star. Huddled all around her. They put a blanket over her. All these White folk never seen a dead body before."

"Did you see where Joanne was shot?"

"In the chest. Maybe in the heart. Hard to tell. She'd be happy it wasn't in the face. She's the kind of girl who'd want an open casket. Three inches of makeup, a new do and a goddamn purple dress."

"Does Mr. Cray know all the things Joanne was up to?"

"I don't know what you're talking about." I raised an eyebrow, until she said, "She's careful. Was careful. She kept all of that out of here. The walls are thin."

That made me wonder if Claudia had heard any of the conversation I'd had with Joanne twenty-four hours ago. Then I wondered if Mr. Cray had heard it.

"How thin? Every single word or just the highlights?"

"Highlights."

I remembered Joanne turning on the radio while we were talking. What had I said that made her do that? I remembered using the words 'kill' and 'murder' a lot more than you would in a typical conversation. I might have mentioned she was embezzling at some point. And then I recalled she'd mentioned explaining me to Mr. Cray when he stuck his head in. How much had she explained? Could it have had something to do with what happened?

"How long did Mr. Cray and Joanne know each other?"

"Forever."

"They were in Sault Sainte Marie for the weekend? They went gambling together?"

That earned another snort. "Yeah. They called it business trips. They'd charge everything to the company and it'd get deducted from his taxes. But yeah, they're just gambling and whatever... Mrs. Cray calls over every time they go someplace, wanting to know the hotel and all that. I have to put on my dumb Black girl act. She buys it every time."

I thanked her and left. I considered asking if I could look around Mr. Cray's office. She didn't seem to like him much so maybe she would have let me. But honestly, I doubted it. She might not mind a little gossip, but actually risking her job—with its obvious benefits—was not a possibility.

I walked to the stairs, went back down to the first floor, and out to the front parking lot. The janitor was still there. He was a White guy just under thirty, tall and slender with crisp blue eyes. When he saw me coming he stopped and leaned on the mop.

"Hey, man," I said, adopting a 'straight' persona. "I knew the woman who was killed. I wonder if you'd answer a few questions." I tried not to look down at the pail full of bloody water.

"You're not a cop?"

"No. I'm not." I'd been smart enough to take a small of wad of the cash Joanne had been collecting. I took it out and peeled off a couple of hundreds, saying as I did, "I'm just a friend of the dead woman's family."

He considered me a moment, and then asked, "What do you wanna know?

"I see there are security cameras," I turned and pointed back at the building, though obviously he knew they were there. "Do you know how I can get copies of the videotape from yesterday?"

He was staring at the money, practically licking his lips. "They don't use tapes anymore. It's all on computer. All that stuff's in a closet on the first floor."

"Do you know how to operate it?"

"I do. I work for JCB. They manage this building, the storage units next door and then two buildings after that. I clean all of them and keep the security cameras running."

"Do any of the buildings have security guards?"

"No, they're all on the discount plan."

"Which is you?"

"Pretty much."

"Can you show me that video from yesterday?"

He shook his head. "Police took the whole computer. Somebody from the company is supposed to bring a new one by later."

"Did you see the recording of what happened?"

"Not much. I mean, I got it running for the cops and then they kind of pushed me out of the way."

"What did you get to see?"

He brightened, clearly thinking this might earn him the money. "They got the guy on video. That's for sure. He was wearing a hoodie. Walked out the front door, shot the lady, took her purse, then looked around like something scared the crap out of him and he ran back toward the building."

That sounded like he saw the whole thing.

"So he came out of the building and ran back into the building?"

"Yeah. That's what the cops were saying. I didn't get to actually see it myself."

"Where were you when the shooting happened?"

"Unstopping a toilet on the first floor. Ladies room."

"Did you hear anything that might be helpful around the time of the murder?"

"I was kind of busy. It was really gross, you know."

I tried not to think about it. I glanced again at the pail with Joanne's diluted blood floating around, and gave him the two hundred bucks. He hadn't told me all that much, but his life sounded disgusting and I figured he deserved the money.

As I started to walk away, he said, "My name's Rocky. I do a twelve-hour shift, Monday through Thursday. Seven to seven. The last hour gets a little dull." There was a glint in his eyes that I recognized.

"Oh. Really... um, I'm flattered. I really am. It's been a while. I have a partner, though."

He pushed his cheek out with his tongue in a very suggestive way and said, "That's too bad. I guess I'll just be bored then."

"Sorry about that."

"If you change your mind, I always spend the last hour next door. First bay."

I didn't really know what he meant by that so I just smiled. And said, "Well, I'm going to take off."

Afterward, just a little impressed with myself, I walked around the building again. The guy in the hoodie came out of the building. That little phrase meant a lot. I jumped to the conclusion that the target was Joanne. Not a big jump, really. But if the killer was really after her car he'd have been in the parking lot watching the car, waiting for the driver. It sounded like he followed Joanne out of the building. Like he was waiting for her.

He followed her out of the building, shot her and went back in. Then what? He'd have to get rid of the hoodie and the gun. Then, once a crowd of people had formed, he could join the crowd, then eventually return to the vehicle he'd come in.

On the east side of the building, there was a narrow parking lot, and a patch of grass between the lot and the storage company next door. I walked the length of the building, looking closely at the grass. My guess was the killer was a least a little familiar with the building. He knew there were cameras, since he was wearing a hoodie, and he knew where they were. So it was likely he'd parked a vehicle on the east side of the building where there wasn't a camera. Or he'd parked in the lot for the storage units next door and walked across. Or he'd driven into the lot and then across the relatively level grass to leave via a different parking lot. None of that was supported by the grass, though. I didn't see any evidence of footprints or tire tracks. The grass looked completely undisturbed.

Then I walked around to the back of the building. There was a bit of landscaping. Prickly bushes, but they weren't difficult to get behind. The camera was aimed at the cars, so if you stayed close to the wall and got behind the bushes you could have entered and left the building unnoticed.

I went back in. The building was very quiet. Claudia was probably right when she said there were a lot of empty offices. I walked the hallway until I got to the rest rooms at the front. I went into the men's. There was a urinal and two stalls, as well as two sinks both with mirrors. There was a paper towel dispenser on the wall and a tall garbage can with a plastic lining.

I took the top off the garbage can and looked down into it. There was very little trash in there, so either the janitor emptied it last night or the police took it. Probably the later.

Then I went into each of the stalls, took the lid off the toilet tank, looked inside, ran my hand around the back and the bottom as best I could. Yes, I'd seen *The Godfather*. No, I did not find the gun. There were not a lot of other places to look.

The ceiling was a drop ceiling, large acoustic-style tile resting on a metal frame. I lifted the flimsy lid on one of the toilets and then, carefully placing my feet, I stood up, clinging to the stall walls and reached up to pop a tile. Sliding the tile to one side, I felt around. Nothing. Nothing was hidden up there. I got down and then checked the tile over the other toilet.

I was out of places to search, so I went into the ladies room next door and repeated the whole process. Nothing. Nada. Then I went up to the second floor. In the men's room, which was the same as the one downstairs, the first thing I noticed was that on the tile over the stall closest to the wall there were a number of dirty handprints. I opened the stall and saw that there was fingerprint powder everywhere, including the tile above my head. There was no reason to search the rest of bathroom.

The police had already been there and they'd found something hidden in the ceiling. The hoodie or the gun or both. I stood there thinking for a bit. I was roughly six-foot three-inches. The toilet was about eighteen inches at the seat. That was seven feet nine inches. Add an inch or so for my shoes, seven foot ten. My arm was about two and a half feet. Over ten feet total.

I guessed the ceiling hung at about nine feet from the floor. I could have probably touched it if I tried. So... How short could someone be and, standing on the toilet, manage to get a gun and/or a hoodie up into the ceiling? Probably as short as five foot four, give or take. Which meant pretty much anyone, and that didn't tell me anything.

Back in the Thunderbird, I sat for a moment thinking about what I'd learned. The police had a video of the killing. They had at least one piece of physical evidence, the hoodie or the gun. They might have fingerprints, they also might not. Most of this had not been released to the press.

It didn't support the idea of this being a random carjacking gone wrong.

CHAPTER NINETEEN

W ho am I? I needed to decide who I was. I'd managed to gloss
over the whole name thing when we'd talked to people, but I
knew I couldn't walk into a room full of people and not give
them a name. Obviously, I wasn't Dom Reilly. Was it safe to be Charles
Henderson?

The police weren't investigating the family. Or at least not yet. They'd
decided a Black kid had killed Joanne. But that could change. What if they
started asking questions about the family and my name came up? What
should that name be?

Charles Henderson had recently flown to Los Angeles and never came
back to Detroit. Cass Reilly had flown from Los Angeles to Reno and
then to Detroit. There were no records as to how he'd gotten to Los
Angeles.

It was okay that I was registered in a motel as Charles Henderson and
that I rented a car under that name. As long as I didn't go introducing
myself to Cass's family as Charles, that name should never come up in an
invest—

Oh shit. I'd made a mistake. A big one. Cass had flown to Reno, flown to Detroit with Dom Reilly. That was bad. Really bad. I needed to do some work covering that up. I needed to have a long conversation with Cass.

Before I got out of the car, I decided it might be smart to drive around the block. I drove to the end of the street and turned right. Approaching the next block, I slowed so I could look down the street and not have to—yup, as expected there was the white van. The Chevy Suburban was probably in front of it. I didn't worry about whether it was actually there. Seeing the van there was enough.

I kept going forward and then worked my way back to Cass's house in such a way that the Feds couldn't see me. I parked a half block away from the house and walked down. Cass's Belvedere sat in the driveway, seeming not to have moved since the last time I'd been there. The Voyager was there again, parked on the street this time, as was the blue Corvette. There seemed to be more Sedan DeVilles than there had been the night before.

Getting to the front door, I rang the bell. After a few moments Aunt Suzie answered. She let me into the foyer, but that was as far as I got before she said, "I called Big Brothers of America. They don't work with any nonprofits who find kids' lost parents."

I put a smile on my face and said, "Sorry about that. Didn't Cass tell you we met in an AOL chatroom about missing relatives. My daughter was missing for two years. Drugs. I was able to find her and get her into rehab. She's doing really well now."

"Is he paying you? That's what he told me."

"He's just paying a few of my expenses."

She searched my face for signs that I was telling the truth.

"You also didn't tell me your name when you came to my house."

"Nick. Nick Nowak." Ironic that after hiding out for eleven years the safest name I could think of was to use was my own.

"Is that short for Dominick?"

"No. Mikolaj."

"Pollack," she said, looking suspicious again. "Pollacks say No-vack, not No-wack."

"Yeah, well my grandparents got tired of having our name spelled wrong all the time so they started using a more American pronunciation." It was the truth, but I wasn't sure she believed me. I distracted her with, "How is Cass doing?"

"He was crying a lot last night. But this morning he's gone silent. He's upstairs in his bedroom."

I glanced into the living room. There were three older men sitting on the couches. Joanne's father and uncles, I assumed. With them was a younger guy in his mid-thirties. He looked completely bereft, his eyes red and swollen. He sniffed and held a hand over his face, trying not to keep crying. The older man next to him slapped the back of his head and said something in Italian.

"I'm going up to see Cass" I said to Aunt Suzie as I went up the stairs. When I got to his bedroom door I didn't knock, I just opened it. He lay on his bed in a pair of ill-fitting black slacks and a white dress shirt.

I put a finger over my lips and nodded toward the bathroom. I turned and went back into the hallway toward the shared bathroom. Luckily, he followed me. When we were in, I closed the door and turned on the water. Quickly, I glanced out the window. I could see the van sitting in the next block.

"What are you doing?"

"The Feds are following your second cousin Luca. Their van is right out there," I pointed to it through the window. "I'm guessing they've got some kind of parabolic microphone aimed at the house. They might have bugged the place, too. Though I'm not sure he's been seeing enough of your mother lately that they could get a warrant."

"What the fuck?" He looked out the window at the van.

"Yeah, what the fuck," I repeated, hoping that closed the subject. "We have a lot to talk about. I just told your aunt we met in an AOL chatroom about missing family members. I told her I had a daughter who was into drugs, but I found her and got her into rehab. Can you remember that?"

"I guess."

"What have the police told you?"

"That it was some Black kid trying to steal the Eldorado."

"That's not true. I'm pretty sure it was someone who—"

"No. It was some Black kid. The police said so. You have to find that kid."

"It's not logical that we were trying to find out who killed your dad and then your mom gets killed randomly. No. Something we did led to this."

"No—"

"Think. Think about what makes sense."

"I can't! You're saying I killed my own mom!"

Oh shit. That was a road I didn't want to go down. "No, that's not what I mean. You didn't kill your mom. You had no way of knowing what might happen if we looked for your dad's killer. Okay? None of this is your fault."

He stood there, absorbing what I'd said. Then he said, "You have to find out who killed my mom."

"Yeah, something told me you were going to say that." I took a deep breath. "The police found something. The killer went back into the building and hid something in the men's room ceiling. Either the gun or the hoodie or maybe your mom's purse. They haven't said anything, have they?"

"No. They came by yesterday and told me she was dead and they think it was a carjacking gone wrong. That's all I've heard."

"You should call them later on today and ask if they know anything else. Then let me know what they say." I told him that I'd moved to the corporate flophouse and registered as Charles Henderson. Then I asked, "Did they want to know where you were yesterday at five o'clock?"

"I said I was picking up Chinese food for dinner."

"And you didn't mention me?"

"No."

"What else did they ask?"

"Nothing really."

"They didn't ask about your mom's love life or if she had any enemies?"

"It wasn't Luca."

"Why do you say that?"

"You think he killed my dad. And maybe... But there's no way he killed my mom. He's really upset. He keeps crying. More than me even."

I didn't think it was Luca either, but not because he was crying. The Feds were watching him. They wouldn't just watch him kill a woman and not do anything about it.

"Tell me about the gun you gave me. It belongs to Luca, doesn't it?"

"Kind of."

"Kind of? What does that mean?"

"He buried it in our backyard. He didn't think we knew about it, but my mom figured it out, dug it up, and brought it into the house."

That wasn't exactly what he'd told me before. Before he'd said Luca gave it to his mother to keep. I said, "So he did something bad with the gun. Do you know what that is?"

He shrugged. "My grandfather was in some trouble. But then the judge got shot in a robbery and we got a better judge. It was around that time."

"Is the gun registered to him?"

"No. That would be dumb. He had a girl he knew buy it."

That was not much smarter. He could still easily be traced to the gun. "Why did your mother dig it up?"

Cass looked embarrassed. "Insurance."

If she needed insurance then she was afraid of Luca. Or someone who cared about Luca. "Has Luca said anything to you about the gun?"

Cass shook his head.

"If he does, let me know."

Abruptly, there was a knock on the door. I jumped. "Shit."

I turned off the water. We were going to look pretty suspicious when we walked out of the bathroom together. I opened the door, just to get it over with.

Aunt Suzie glowered at me. "What are the two of you doing?"

I made a snap decision, pulled her into the bathroom and turned the water pack on. "The Feds are investigating Luca, they've got a microphone aimed at the house."

"How do you know that?"

"Their van is in the next block. You can see it out the window. It's white."

She walked over and looked out the window. Then she said, "Okay. What does this have to do with the two of you?"

"He's Cass's cousin. I thought he should know."

"Are you going to tell Luca?" she asked Cass.

"I don't know. Should I?"

"I want you to think about coming to live with me. You need to stay away from your mother's family as best you can."

"She's right, Cass. You should do that."

She looked at me suspiciously even though I was agreeing with her. And she had every reason to look at me that way.

"They loved my mom. They love me."

"That doesn't mean they're good for you," I said. "Love doesn't always work that way."

"That doesn't make sense," he said reflexively. I suspect it made more sense to him than he wanted it to.

Aunt Suzie turned the water off, effectively ending our conversation. She opened the door and left the bathroom. Cass and I followed her downstairs.

Little had changed in the living room. Everyone was silent. Aunt Suzie excused herself and slipped by us, going to the kitchen. There was an awkward moment, and then I elbowed Cass.

"Oh. Yeah. This is my friend..."

"Nick Nowak," I said.

He glanced at me, he'd not heard the name before, then he continued, "Nick, this is my great grandfather Salvatore Di Stefano, my grandfather Gianni Di Stefano and my great uncle Fredo Amato, and my second cousin Luca Amato."

Uncle Fredo was the one who'd slapped Luca in the back of the head earlier.

"You have my condolences," I said. None of them seemed to hear me.

Luca sniffed, and then asked, "Who are you? Where did you come from?"

Neither question was the one he wanted answered, I trotted out my cover story. "I met Cass in a chatroom on AOL about missing people. I'm trying to help him find out what happened to his dad."

That caught Fredo's attention and he turned to glare at me, but it was Gianni who said, "He ran off. The piece of shit. Left my helpless little girl alone with a baby."

Our brief acquaintance had told me Joanne was anything but helpless.

"We're trying to figure out where he ran off to. Cass would like to see his father again."

Attention shifted to Cass, who said, "Yeah... I would... like to."

Strangely, Gianni just shrugged. He knew we'd never find Dominick Reilly and he seemed to not care if we tried. I said, "If you have any ideas about where he might be..."

Even Cass understood what a dangerous thing that was to say. He said, "Let's get some food, okay?" He led me across the foyer to the dining room where the table was already covered in food, mainly cookies.

I wondered if the Feds had gotten most of the conversation in the living room. Then I wondered if that would be a good thing or a bad thing. For one thing, I'd used my real name. Was that a bad thing? Maybe not. There had to be a hundred Nick Nowak's in the country. And this Nick Nowak could disappear, and would, at a moment's notice.

A woman in her early thirties came out of the kitchen carrying a platter of cookies.

"Aunt Josette, this is my friend, Nick," Cass said.

She moved a few things, set down the platter, wiped her hands on her apron then extended one to shake. I shook it. Then she pointed to the table and explained, "Pignoli, amaretti, pizzelles, butter cookies, anisette. There will be real food out in a bit."

I picked up a paper plate and picked out a few cookies. Aunt Josette was watching me. Defensively, I smiled.

"Did you come by the bakery? I heard someone was asking questions."

"Ah, yes. That was me."

"No, Vicky said the guy was named Charles. Are you Charles?"

"Sometimes it's good not to leave your name, you know?"

"If you're up to no good, it certainly is."

This conversation needed a change of direction, so I said, "I enjoyed the biscotti I bought. Are these the same kind?"

"Biscotti," she corrected my pronunciation emphasizing the strong 'o' sound in the middle. "What exactly were you trying to find out?"

"Cass wants to know what happened to his dad. Your coworker said you think Joanne had him killed. That you though she was a narcissistic whore."

She had the decency to look embarrassed by that. To Cass she said, "Oh honey, you know what happened to your dad. Everyone knows what happened to him." She lowered her voice, and said, "His killer is sitting in the living room. I wouldn't be surprised if..."

Cass said, "Luca seems really upset."

Aunt Josette shrugged. "Yeah, it seems genuine. But that's men... crying about messes they've made themselves."

CHAPTER TWENTY

September 17, 1996
Tuesday afternoon

We followed Aunt Josette into the kitchen. The room was filled with women, mostly older. There seemed to be two old women for every old man in the living room. They wore somber colors and simple aprons. It suggested a Hollywood depiction of women from a small Sicilian village. Right and wrong at the same time.

The kitchen itself was transformed. Suddenly, there was everything you needed to make a feast for hundreds. Obviously, they'd brought it all with them. If Joanne had been hiding it all somewhere, I hadn't found it.

Cass introduced me to the women. I couldn't keep their names straight two minutes after I'd been told. One of them was in her late thirties, tall, thin and beak-nosed. A cousin. Bella? Della? She seemed to be doing nothing but cutting onions, her eyes red from it. One of the old women poked her. Presumably to get her to talk to me, since I was the subject at hand. She pushed the other woman's hand away.

I was offered wine, something called rosso. I turned it down and had a lemon soda forced on me. Bella was made to give it to me.

"You have a wife?" the oldest woman in the room asked.

To put an end to the Bella's misery and to go along with my cover story, I said, "Yes. Yes I do."

The old woman said, "Hmmmphf." As though my being married was a personality flaw. I imagine I'd have been stabbed with a kitchen knife if I'd mentioned my longtime boyfriend.

I stuffed my mouth with cookies, hoping I wouldn't be asked any more questions. That didn't stop them from staring baldly at me.

Aunt Suzie stood at the stove stirring a large pot. One of the other women reached for a jar of spice and was about to shake some in when Suzie stopped her.

"No, no, no... It's lamb stew. You don't put oregano in there."

"Basil?"

As she waved the woman away, I heard the doorbell ring. Someone was arriving. I stood close to the swinging door in hopes of hearing who it might be. I heard a man go to the door, I think it might have been Luca. Another man said a few things. Then the door shut and their voices got further away.

Cass tapped me on the shoulder, and I followed him out onto the patio where I'd spoken with Joanne about thirty-six hours before. Not even two days. Carla and Rose Amato were out there, looking tense and seemingly in exile.

When she saw me, Carla said, "You know, neither Rose nor I could remember your name after you left. Why do you think that is?"

"Oh, well... it's Nick," I said, as though saying my name was the easiest, most natural thing in the world. "I'm sure I told you."

I hadn't, but better to make her think she'd forgotten something than for her to think I wasn't telling her something.

"Did you ever find your card? You said it was in your other jeans."

"That was a little fib. I'm not actually a private detective."

"Shocking," she said, dry again. As dry as a summer breeze in Palm Springs.

"I met Cass in an AOL chatroom about finding missing relatives."

"Who are you missing?" she asked me.

"My daughter. Thankfully, I found her. She's doing well. Back in school. After that experience, I felt like I should help others."

"It's so terrible what happened to your mom," Rose said. "How can you bear it, Cassidy? You must be destroyed."

Not really the kind of thing you should say to someone who's probably destroyed. The boy made a strangled sound, so I said, "He's doing remarkably well. He's thinking about going to stay with his Aunt Suzie."

"The Di Stefano's will hate that," Carla said. I could swear she almost smiled.

"Why aren't the two of you in the kitchen helping out?"

"We're feminists."

To Cass I said, "You've got a couple of aunts in the kitchen. Is one of them..."

"Yes, one of them is our mother," Carla said. "What does that have to do with your finding Dominick Reilly?"

"Carla, we shouldn't have come here," Rose said. "You know they don't want us around. You know they think we're liars." To me she said, "We're not liars. We would never lie."

"Don't say anything else, Rose." Carla stood up. "We only came because of you, Cassidy. If you need anything let me know, we'll do what we can."

Rose stood up. "Can we go around the side? I don't want to walk through the house."

"Of course we can." To me, she said, "Our little family dramas have nothing to do with whatever happened to Dominick."

Then they walked around the side of the house. When they were out of earshot, I asked Cass, "Do you know what's going on with them? I have the feeling it has something to do with their brother, Luca."

"I think he used to do stuff to them."

"What stuff?"

"You know... stuff."

"Like the stuff he used to do with your mom?"

First cousins weren't supposed to mess around. It wasn't a big leap to think he'd done the same sort of thing with his sister. But that didn't seem to be it, Cass gave me a confused look, and said, "I don't think he ever beat up my mom."

Violence, bullying, maybe more. Whatever happened it wasn't going to go away. The two women who'd just left weren't going to let it go away.

Cass was standing there very still, like he was making an effort not to move. At that moment, he was like a fawn in the woods being hunted. If he stayed quiet, didn't make a move, grief might not find him. But it would find him. It found us all.

"They're wrong, you know. About my mom."

"Who's wrong?"

"Josette. And, well, everybody. They didn't know her like I did. She was scared mostly. She didn't think she was pretty or smart or anything, really. She didn't think anyone liked her. There was no one to love her. Except me."

I wasn't sure how much of that I believed. It did explain the Xanax. If she told all that to a psychiatrist and added a few tears she'd likely have gotten a prescription. It sounded like manipulation. But then, I had to admit that people often used the truth to manipulate others. Maybe she did feel all those things and only ever talked about them when it was to her benefit.

I still had to say something to Cass about all this. I went with, "You were a good son. I'm sure she knew that."

He wiped his nose. I could tell he was trying not to cry. Without much thought, I said, "None of this is going to help, you know."

"What are you talking about?"

"Finding out what happened to your dad, finding out who killed your mom. It won't help with the pain you're feeling. It's going to hurt like hell no matter what happens."

"Why do you have to say shit like that?"

He walked into the house. Which I suppose was a good thing because I didn't really have an answer to his question. Did I really think telling him how shitty things were going to get would help him? Weren't we all better off pretending things were better than they were no matter how bad they got?

No. I didn't think we were.

I decided the best thing to do would be to eat. I went back inside, hoping they'd put out something that wasn't a hundred and fifty percent sugar. I was in luck, a pasta dish had come out, along with an antipasto. I picked up a paper plate—the good kind that didn't flop—and waited in the short line. I watched as two of the older women filled plates and then brought them over to the living room.

When it was my turn, I filled the plate with cheese and meats from the antipasto and took a healthy serving of the pasta dish which was rigatoni in a red sauce with eggplant. The dining chairs had been pushed up against the walls, so I sat down in one and started eating.

I wondered where Cass had gotten to. I was tempted to set aside my lunch and go find him, but it might not be a good idea to seem so attached to him. Heaven forbid people got the wrong idea. Actually heaven forbid they got the right idea.

Was I any closer to getting myself out of this mess? It made sense that whoever killed Joanne also killed her husband. That *did* make sense, didn't it? Someone helped her get rid of Dominick. My asking around with Cass had caused that person to kill Joanne. Had they thought she would tell?

Wait. Given my brief experience of the woman, knowing someone was looking into her husband's disappearance wouldn't have caused her to confess... It would have caused her to demand something of the killer. Even if that killer was doing her bidding.

That raised an issue I hadn't thought about much: What if Joanne didn't ask that her husband be killed? What if she knew who did it but wasn't involved? Honestly, that didn't make a lot of sense.

Which brought me back to Luca. He probably killed the real Dom Reilly. But he probably didn't kill Joanne. He was being followed by the Feds, they wouldn't have just watched him kill Joanne, they'd have arrested him. He'd be in an interview room right now turning state's evidence on whoever he had to—probably the old men in the living room—to make his life easier.

From where I was sitting, I could almost hear the conversation in the living room. I heard Mr. Cray saying "...believe this has happened. I left... after she...driven right by and not ... anything."

I didn't quite hear the answers to that but they seemed kind. He was getting a much warmer reception than I'd gotten. And then they were talking about money. The number six thousand kept coming up. They were talking about whether the stock market would get over six thousand. Mr. Cray said it would never happen if Clinton won the election. That caused a bit of spirited discussion, Joanne's family being Catholic and democrats.

That made me think of home. Ronnie was very engaged in the upcoming election. He'd put a Clinton sign in our window, was threatening to canvas, and had begun arguing about Don't Ask, Don't Tell with our friends—some of whom felt betrayed. I was planning not to vote—

without letting Ronnie know that. It wasn't that I didn't have opinions, it was more that we already knew California would go for Clinton so my one vote didn't matter much. And if it didn't matter, I didn't see a reason to add voter fraud to my list of crimes.

I'd just about finished my pasta and was deciding whether I should get more—I definitely wanted more of the lemon soda—when there was a rushing noise from the living room and something fell over. Something else broke. Voices were raised. I stepped into the foyer so I could better see what was happening.

Luca had Mr. Cray shoved up against the wall. An end table had fallen over and a lamp lay broken on the floor. One of the furniture store land-scapes hung crookedly over Cray's head.

Two of the old men had gotten up and were yelling at Luca to stop. His forearm was across Cray's throat and he was pressing. Cray's hands were attempting to pull Luca's arm away. Cass stood behind a chair looking confused.

I wondered if I should step in. I was one of the younger people in the room. But Cass's grandfather and great uncle were in the way. And then, Salvatore Di Stefano—still on the sofa—said, "Luca. No."

Reluctantly, Luca released Mr. Cray, letting him slide a few inches down the wall. The man tried to recapture his dignity. He adjusted his clothes and said, "Really, I meant nothing disrespectful. And I'm sorry if you took it that way."

Luca returned to his former seat. He did not look appeased. The old men sat down. Mr. Cray looked around and, wisely I thought, said "I really should be leaving. My family, they're upset, of course. It could have happened to anyone."

He walked out of the living room, passed me and went out the front door. I managed to catch Cass's eye. I nodded my head toward the back of the house. Then I turned and walked back through the dining room, through the raucous kitchen—where they seemed to have missed the fight in the living room completely—and out into the garage.

The garage was empty. Joanne's car had been impounded somewhere. Cass was right behind me. I turned to him and asked, "What happened in there?"

"Mr. Cray said that he'd told Mom not to be so flashy. Luca said that sounded like he was blaming the whole thing on her. Then he rushed at Mr. Cray and everything got crazy."

"Do you think that's all there was to it?"

"What do you mean? That's what they said."

"People don't always say what they mean. I've gotten the impression your mom might have had something going on with her cousin and then maybe with Mr. Cray."

"My mom wasn't a slut."

"I didn't say that. And believe me, I'm not one to talk."

He looked like he was trying not to think about that last bit. I went on, "Look, I'm going to go soon. Do you know where Mr. Cray lives?"

"In Novi. Not far from the office. Bellagio Drive. Are you going to talk to him?"

"No. I might drive by tomorrow. Get a sense of who he is."

"He's kind of an asshole, to be honest. But I don't think you'll be able to figure that out from his front lawn."

"You'd be surprised what I can figure out from someone's front lawn."

We were quiet a moment. I had the feeling the whole thing was hitting the kid, and hitting him hard. Half to distract him and half out of curiosity, I asked, "How come you haven't put your car in here? It's a classic. You want it to stay safe."

He looked sheepish for a moment, then said, "My mom wouldn't like it."

CHAPTER TWENTY-ONE

September 17, 1996
Tuesday late afternoon

I left after that, driving straight to Top Dog. It was around two o'clock. Maybe two-thirty. I wasn't sure if the clock on the Thunderbird's dashboard was correct. It was in the mid-sixties, warm enough to make the jacket I'd purchased uncomfortable. I didn't take it off, though. It was the only way to carry the gun.

Entering the building, it was just a bit warmer than it was outside. In the lobby they had one of those ugly black directories, the kind with white plastic letters that clip into grooves and make it easy to swap out when the businesses fail. I read through the list of companies, searching for one that sounded like their business was re-insurance. It took a moment, but I settled on National Casualty. They were in suite 108.

Walking down the hall, I tried to think about what I needed to learn. But it was basically anything you could tell me at that point. I found the right door, opened it, and stepped in. The set-up was similar to Top Dog. A truncated reception area with a desk and two offices. No—they had three. Still, small. I wondered how national their casualties could be.

There was a girl at the reception desk who was little more than a teenager.

"Hello. I was told that someone in this office witnessed the shooting yesterday. Do you know anything about that?"

"It wasn't me."

An older woman stepped out of one of the offices. A plaque next to the door said LOIS SITWELL. Lois was around fifty, not very tall and a bit round in the middle.

"It was me," she said. "Who are you?"

"I'm a friend of the woman's family. They've asked me to look into this."

I was avoiding using my name again. If I had to I would, but it seemed better to breeze right by it.

With a scowl, she said, "Isn't that what the police are for?"

"Joanne's family is concerned they won't do their best."

Using Joanne's name was a good idea, since Lois relaxed a tiny bit. She said, "I didn't see very much and I wish people would stop asking me about it."

"What did you see?"

"I was leaving. Walking to my car. It was in the front parking lot. I was getting in when I heard the pop. It was loud. I wasn't sure what was happening at first. My first thought was hunters, actually."

"In Novi?" the girl said, skeptically.

"I didn't say it was a rational thought. Anyway, I saw the kid running away, then I walked around the car and saw the woman, Joanne, lying on the ground."

"You saw the kid? You saw that he was a Black kid?"

"Not exactly."

"So you didn't get a good look?"

"I saw the hooded sweatshirt he was wearing. You know, that's the kind of thing they wear. And... well, he stole her purse."

"But you never saw his hands or any part of his face?"

"It was the policeman, he said..."

But I could tell from her face that she couldn't remember him actually saying the kid was Black. Likely he'd implied it enough to get her to agree. She had the decency to be embarrassed by her mistake.

"Tell me anything about the hoodie. What color was it?"

"Green."

"Spartan green,' the girl said. "That's what you said."

"Yes. It was Spartan green."

"What kind of green is that?" I asked. The girl giggled.

The woman said, "You're not from Michigan, are you?"

"No. I'm not."

"Michigan State. Spartans."

I remembered something about the real Spartans being gay warriors. I decided this was not the time to bring that up.

Finally, the woman felt pity on me and said, "It's a very specific dark green."

"You think the killer is a student?" I asked.

"Oh, God no. Michigan State is up in Lansing."

"So the killer's brother or sister goes there?"

"Not likely. People just wear the gear. They're fans probably. College football."

"The Wolverines are yellow," the girl added.

"University of Michigan. There's a rivalry. U of M is over in Ann Arbor. People down here tend to lean toward the Wolverines. But there's a healthy dose of Spartan fans. You can buy their gear at K-Mart. Especially at this time of year. The game is next month."

"So the hoodie doesn't tell us anything," I said, disappointed.

"You asked what color it was. It tells you that."

She was right, but for a moment I'd thought the color might tell me more.

"Did the kid in the hoodie make any attempt to steal the car?"

"Not that I saw, no. But then he might have before."

"Is there anything else you remember that might be useful?"

"It all happened very quickly. I barely knew what was happening until it was over. "She might have said, 'Why?'"

"Really? You think she asked 'why'?"

"I wasn't looking in that direction so I can't be sure. I might be imagining that part. I mean, if someone was going to kill me in a parking lot, I think I'd ask why. So maybe that's why I think I heard it."

"Or you heard it."

"Yes, I could have."

I thanked her and left. As I walked around I wondered about the word 'why'. Did that mean Joanne knew her killer and wanted to know why he was about to shoot her? Or was it a question she asked a stranger?

I leaned toward the former. She knew her killer. A stranger there to steal your things didn't need an explanation. But someone you knew, someone you thought cared about you, that did raise the question of 'why?'

I figured it was around three fifteen. I wandered around the building and then went outside. I had two main suspects: Luca and Mr. Cray. Neither made much sense.

Luca was being followed by the Feds so that made his committing murder seem unlikely. But then I remembered the first time I saw the Feds they were sitting outside Luca's Lifters and Luca was nowhere to be found. So he might have given them the slip. That was even more plausible if he knew he was being followed by the Feds. Did he know? Was there a way to find out if he knew?

And then there was Mr. Cray. He might have overheard my conversation with Joanne that afternoon. He might have overheard that she was embezzling from him. Hell, she might have gone into his office afterwards and demanded something from him the way she'd demanded something from me. I couldn't be sure. But what I could be sure of was that if Mr. Cray decided to kill Joanne that afternoon, he didn't leave himself much time to plan the murder. He'd have to have had a gun right there in the office. The same with the hoodie; it would have to have been in his office. He'd have needed to hide the gun and the hoodie as he walked passed Claudia, go somewhere to put on the hoodie, then proceed out of the building, and shoot Joanne. Then he'd have to reverse the process: Hide something in the ceiling of the men's room on the second floor and then go out to his car at the back of the building. I wasn't sure there was time for all of that. In fact, I was pretty sure there wasn't.

Of course, either of them could have hired someone to kill Joanne. Was that plausible? Could Mr. Cray have done it that afternoon? Could you order a killer the way you could a pizza?

I was outside on the east side of the building, the side without cameras, when I noticed something. The building next door. The storage place. There were cameras on each corner of that building. And they were pointed at the building I was standing next to. They'd have been recording everything that happened on that side of the building.

I began moving with more purpose. I needed to find Rocky, the janitor. He didn't seem to be anywhere in the building with Top Dog, so I walked over to the storage place, circled the building and then moved on.

The next two buildings were very similar to the one that housed Top Dog. Both were two stories and wide, with lots of parking lot. I found Rocky on the first floor of the first building. He smiled when he saw me, a little too big.

"I have more questions," I said quickly, not wanting him to get the wrong idea.

"That's disappointing."

I took a couple hundred dollars out of my pocket, and said, "Not that disappointing."

I handed the money over right away. He might not want to help me, but I knew he wouldn't want to give the money back.

"What do you need?"

"The building with the storage units, it has camera's pointed at the first building. Did the police take that computer?"

He shook his head. "No."

"Did you remind them it was pointed at the building where there were no cameras?"

"Oh gosh... must have slipped my mind."

"Have you looked at it already?"

"Yeah."

"Can you show it to me?"

He shrugged. He probably wasn't supposed to. "Yeah, sure, why not. You'll be disappointed though. It doesn't show much."

"Okay, well, let's look at it anyway."

We walked back to the storage building. At the front, one of the bays had been converted into a security room. They'd lined it with unpainted sheetrock, and cut a door and a window into what had been a roll-up door. There were large metal tubes leading to vents across the ceiling. There was some kind of heater/air conditioner somewhere outside.

At the furthest end of the room was a banquet table with a couple of stand-up computers beneath it and several monitors on the table, along with a keyboard. One monitor was dedicated to the operation of the computer, the other monitors showed what was being recorded. Based on what I was seeing, there were eight cameras installed around the building we were in. More than the building where Top Dog was located.

"Why does this building have more cameras?" I asked.

"Bigger target. People get it in their heads storage units are filled with hidden treasures. They're not. It's mainly just people's junk."

Scanning the monitors, I picked out the two cameras that were aimed at the building next door. They would be the most useful.

"Can you go back to yesterday around four-forty-five?"

"Sure." He called up the interface program that allowed him to control the cameras. Clicked in a few numbers and a short time later we were looking at yesterday.

There were two views that mattered. The one of the southwest camera, and the one from the northwest camera. The south camera took in part of the parking lot next door where the shooting took place. The parking lot wasn't even a third full. I could easily pick out Joanne's Cadillac.

The video was black-and-white, with a time code running across the top. The Cadillac, which in real life was bronze, read as a pale gray. We began watching at 4:30.

"I can fast forward if you want," Rocky said.

"Let me get oriented first."

An older man walked out of the building and got into a Ford Taurus and drove away. As he left the parking lot, a minivan drove in and parked. No one got out. They must be picking someone up, I thought. Nothing happened for a bit.

"You like living here?" I asked Rocky to fill the time. "In Detroit?"

"Not really sure. It's the only place I've ever been. Grew up here."

"Maybe you should get out and see the world. You're still a young guy."

"Yeah, maybe I should," he said in a way that made me think he wouldn't. I wondered why. But then I watched a woman come out of the building. She wore a leather jacket that looked like Joanne's purple one. It was very dark on the video. I was pretty sure it was Joanne even though the quality of the video made faces hard to distinguish. She stopped, looked through her purse, and then pulled out a cigarette. She lit it and inhaled deeply. After studying the cloudy sky for a moment, she walked to the Cadillac.

She didn't get in, though. She stood there smoking. Which made sense. Joanne was a woman who didn't smoke in her own house to spare the drapes. Standing outside her car to smoke made sense. It also might have gotten her killed.

The kid in the hoodie came out of the building. On the video, the hoodie was so dark it looked black. When he got close to Joanne, he pulled something out of the hoodie's pouch. The gun. It only took a second and he shot her.

"Can I see that again?"

Rocky ran the video back. I watched the murder a second time. This time, I picked out Lois Sitwell. She'd come out of the building about forty seconds after Joanne and walked to a Lincoln Continental sedan—though it might have been a Crown Vic, it was hard to tell in the video. She was looking at the door handle as the gun went off. She ducked—well, squatted really. She hadn't mentioned that. By the time she stood up the shooter was entering the building. She barely got a look at him at all.

"Again?"

Rocky ran the video backward. This time I watched Joanne. Yes, Joanne might have said, 'Why?' It looked as if her lips had moved. The cigarette dropped to the ground right before she was shot. She knew what was happening.

"Is there a way to enlarge the picture?"

"Not really. The cameras record at seventy-two dpi."

"What is dpi?"

"Dots per inch."

"That doesn't sound like a lot."

"It's not. When you enlarge that kind of image, the computer puts a pixel in between. It kind of guesses. Garbage in garbage out. That's what they say. Did you want to see it again?"

"Yes. Let's let it play all the way through this time."

I kept an eye on the second screen this time. It covered the back parking lot, which was pretty quiet. Looking back to the first screen, the Ford Taurus drove out of the parking lot. The minivan arrived and parked. We waited.

There was a young woman at the edge of the back parking lot. I hadn't noticed her before. She was looking at something in her hand, probably a flip phone. Then she was holding it up in the air. She was trying to find bars.

I looked back at the front parking lot. Joanne came out of the building at 4:51. She looked into her purse, fished out a pack of her long skinny cigarettes, and lit one. Lois Sitwell came out of the building and squeezed past Joanne, brushing smoke away from her face as she did. It was 4:53.

Joanne walked to her car, stood next to it, and smoked. Lois Sitwell's Lincoln was closer to the road, facing in the opposite direction of Joanne's Cadillac. Lois was standing next to the driver's door. At first it seemed that she was just staring at the door, but then I realized she was trying to enter a code to open the vehicle. Those cars had a five button keypad above the door handle and you put a number in to open them.

The shooter came out of the building at 4:55. He walked directly to Joanne. He doesn't decide to steal Joanne's vehicle. He could have gone after Lois's. She'd just gotten the door open. No, he went directly to Joanne and shot her at 4:56. She hadn't even opened her car door yet.

Joanne slumped to the ground. The shooter bent down and took her purse, which was still hooked in her elbow. He ran back to the building and entered it at 4:58. The murder and robbery had taken two minutes.

I continued to watch. Lois walked over to Joanne's body and began screaming. Something caught my eye and I looked at the view of the back of the building. The young woman had gotten bars and was talking. But the screaming made her stop. Then, still talking, she rushed over to a Geo Metro and got in. She drove along the far side of the parking lot, disappearing for ten seconds, and then sped through the front parking lot and out onto the street.

A couple of people had come out of the building. Most people worked until six. One of the perks of dunning poor people for money appeared to be banker's hours. A younger woman was trying to calm Lois down. Funny, in our interview she hadn't mentioned being that upset.

In the back parking lot, Mr. Cray came out of the building carrying a briefcase. It was 5:02. He walked directly to his BMW and then drove out of the parking lot. He passed the front parking lot at 5:04. There were a few people standing around, but not many. Thinking about it for just a moment, it didn't really seem odd that Mr. Cray didn't notice anything unusual.

Then the minivan began to move and drive out of the parking lot at 5:06.

"Stop for a minute."

Rocky paused the images.

"Do you think that minivan could be a Plymouth Voyager?"

"Hard to tell."

"But there on the back bumper. That's a Clinton/Gore bumper sticker, isn't it?"

"It could be."

Suzie. Aunt Suzie. She'd arrived a few minutes before Joanne was shot, sat there in the van and watched her get shot and then drove away. That had to mean she had something to do with it. Didn't it? Had she hired someone to kill Joanne? Who? Who had she gotten to do it?

CHAPTER TWENTY-TWO

September 17, 1996
Tuesday evening

After we fast-forwarded through a couple of hours before the murder and a couple of hours afterward, we watched Joanne get killed a few more times. I was trying to work out where the shooter might have gone. Obviously, he took the hoodie off and stashed it somewhere—possibly in the ceiling of the second-floor men's room. Then where did he go? Did he wait until he heard the police sirens? Did he come out of the building at the same time as the people who worked there? At its height, there was a crowd of twenty or twenty-five people. Even though the building was fully occupied, there were enough different businesses that no one would have noticed someone they didn't recognize. They probably saw people they didn't recognize all the time. Even if you only counted temps and clients.

I looked through the small crowd several times but didn't see anyone who stood out. Not that I could see anyone clearly. The cameras were actually a couple hundred feet away so people were very small. And, as Rocky had explained, the quality was low. The people I did recognize, I recognized partly because of other factors: Joanne's jacket, the Voyager with a bumper sticker, Mr. Cray coming out the back of the building with his briefcase. Any of those could be wrong, except I knew they weren't.

Before I left, I gave Rocky a couple hundred more out of Joanne's stash. He asked me, "Where are you from? You're not from Michigan."

"I'm from California." And as soon as I said it I wished I hadn't. I didn't want people to know that much about me. "San Diego," I lied.

"That's where I'd go. If I was gonna leave. I'd go to California, re-invent myself."

"Not a bad idea."

I drove back to the corporate flophouse. I'd decided to deal with Aunt Suzie in the morning. I hated the idea that she was involved. But she was there and that meant something. It might even mean I got to go home soon.

I missed home. I missed Ronnie. Terribly. We'd only been together a few months when we bought a little house on Bennett and moved in together. It was a crazy thing to do. I nearly backed out three or four times. That would have been logical, but imagining my life without Ronnie has been difficult almost from the moment I met him.

I debated whether to call him. I wanted to wait until I could tell him exactly when I'd be home. He was going to be furious with me... and rightly so.

When I walked into the motel room the phone was ringing. That was disturbing. No one knew where I was. I picked it up and said, "Hello."

"Hey, it's Cass."

Okay, one person knew where I was.

"Hey. What's going on?"

"I need to you to come back to the house, okay?"

"Why?"

"Just come back."

"You can't tell me over the phone?"

"No. I can't."

"Are people still there?"

"Some, yeah."

"Okay. I'll be there in a few minutes."

I hung up. Honestly, I had no idea what that was about. Driving over I weighed the possibilities. He probably had some theory about who killed his mom or his dad or both. Probably one that was way off base.

I wondered if Aunt Suzie would still be there—and whether I should talk to her about what I'd seen. No, I shouldn't talk to her. Not in front of Cass. If she'd hired someone to kill Joanne I didn't want him to know. I didn't want him getting any ideas about—well, I didn't really think he'd kill his aunt. Would he? Oh, God, maybe. No, if she was involved then I needed to convince her to turn herself in. For Cass's sake.

The Voyager was still in front of the house when I got there. The Cadillacs were gone, as was the Corvette. A purple Honda Civic I hadn't seen before sat in the driveway. The Belvedere was gone. I assumed he'd pulled it into the garage.

Before I could ring the doorbell, Cass opened the door. He'd been waiting for me. His eyes looked worried, but all he said was, "Hey."

He walked away and I followed, shutting the front door behind me. The living room and dining room had been cleaned up with everything put back in place. In the kitchen, Aunt Suzie was at the sink washing the few remaining dishes, while Heather sat at the breakfast nook with a very good-looking Hispanic guy about her same age.

"Hello again," Heather said. "This is Hector. He's a friend. I'm sorry, I don't remember your name."

"Nick."

They each had a bowl of Aunt Suzie's stew. I noted that the cans of Diet Coke that had once taken up a shelf in the refrigerator now sat on the counter. I imagined it had been cleaned out to make room for all the food that had been served that afternoon.

Cass was anxious for me to follow him into the garage, and I would have if Suzie hadn't asked, "What brings you back, Nick?"

I didn't have an answer for that. Fortunately, Cass said,

"I called. There's something I want to talk to him about."

To me, Aunt Suzie said, "If you learned anything about what happened to my brother I deserve to know."

"I haven't learned anything you don't already know," I said, without thinking about whether I was being truthful or not. To be honest, I'd almost forgotten about Dom's disappearance completely.

I walked out of the kitchen into the garage. As I'd suspected, Cass had moved the Belvedere into the garage. He opened the driver's door, reached behind the front seat, and pulled out a brown paper bag. He handed it to me and I opened it. Inside was a dark green Spartan's hoodie with a Colt

38 sitting on top of it. The gun was similar to the duty weapon I carried when I was a cop twenty years before. This gun might have been ten or fifteen years old.

"Where was this?"

"Behind the driver's seat."

"And how did you find it?"

"When I pulled the car into the garage, I braked a little fast and the bag hit the back of the seat, making a kind of crinkle noise. I checked it out."

That was when I realized he smelled of alcohol. That explained the 'braked a little fast'. "You've been drinking."

"Yeah, so what?"

"I get it. Your mom just died. Just don't make yourself sick. That wasn't fun, was it?"

He shrugged. "Whatever."

"No. Not whatever. Whoever put this into your car has probably already left an anonymous tip with the police. They're probably getting a warrant and will be here in the morning. Someone wants to pin your mom's murder on you."

"Why would they do that?"

"To protect themselves," I said. "I'm going to take this away. I don't want you caught with it."

"Okay... Do you think it was someone who was here today?"

"I don't know. I suppose someone could have put it into your car sometime during the night. It was outside."

I was well aware that it could have been put there by his aunt. She was there. She watched it happen. She probably paid someone to kill Joanne, and they gave her the hoodie and the gun. And now she's trying... No, that didn't make any sense. I was sure she genuinely cared about her nephew. She might have had Joanne killed, but she wouldn't blame it on Cass. So what was going on?

Even as we stood there, I began planning to visit Aunt Suzie first thing in the morning. Without Cass. "Why don't you open the garage door, and I'll take care of these and see you tomorrow."

"You don't want to come back inside?"

"You go in. Don't have anything else to drink and get some sleep. The cops will be here in the morning, you'll need your wits about you."

"Aunt Suzie wants me to go home with her."

"Try to get her to stay here."

"I'll try," he said, doubtfully as he hit the button to open the garage door. As I walked down the driveway, I realized it might be hard to get Aunt Suzie alone in the morning. I might need to ask her what she was doing at Top Dog in front of Cass. That gave me a queasy feeling in my stomach.

Then I lucked out. I was standing at the trunk of the Thunderbird when I heard the front door close. I turned and saw Aunt Suzie stomping toward me. When she got close, she said, "What were the two of you talking about? I know it's about Dominick. You found something out, didn't you?"

I opened the bag and held it out so she could look into it. "You know what that is, don't you? Someone put it into the back of Cass's Car."

"Someone's trying to blame Cass? But... he was with you, wasn't he? He picked up Chinese food... there will be a credit card receipt, won't there?"

"Yes. But, Cass and his mom had a habit of buying things with other people's cards. So he really can't prove he was there."

"He wasn't at Top Dog though. They can't prove he was."

"You were there though, weren't you?"

"What? No. I wasn't. Of course, I wasn't."

"I watched the security video. A Plymouth Voyager pulled into the parking lot at around forty-thirty and left shortly after Joanne was gunned down. It had a Clinton/Gore sticker on the back."

Okay, so I couldn't be a hundred percent sure of the make of the van or what the bumper sticker said—but her face told me I was right.

A determined look came over her face. "I play softball. In the spring and summer. I have four bats—well, five actually. I put one in the van and I went there. I was going to... I know she killed my brother, her and her cousin. She didn't have to do that. She could have divorced him and the dope would have paid her child support."

"You sat and watched while she got shot?"

"I didn't know that was going to happen. I was going to go over and beat her to death. I had the courage to do it. I did. But then I thought about Cass and... I couldn't do it to him."

"But it happened anyway." I said.

"Did you see who did it?"

"He kept his head down. I don't think even Joanne got a good look at him.

"Did you see anything? What kind of jeans he was wearing? Sneakers? His hands? Anything he had around his neck?"

She thought for a moment before she said, "He wasn't wearing jeans. Just dark slacks. And shoes. Not sneakers."

Okay, that meant something. It could have been any man in the building. "Did he seem at all interested in the car?"

"No. I don't know why they're saying things about a car-jacking. He just grabbed her purse and ran back into the building."

And then ran to the second floor bathroom and put Joanne's purse in the ceiling, but kept the hoodie and the gun. Finally, I shut the trunk of the rental.

"Whoever put that bag in the back of Cass's car has probably already tipped off the police. They're probably getting a warrant right now. Stay here with Cass so he's not alone—"

"I'll bring him to my house."

"No. Someone should be here for the search. Otherwise they'll break the door down. You also want to make sure they only search what's listed on the warrant."

Then she went pale. "Are they going to figure out I was in that parking lot?"

"I haven't seen the footage they have, what I saw came from the building next door. But from what I saw, they couldn't read your license plate. They're also not looking for you. They've got their hearts set on a Black teenager."

She visibly relaxed. Then she said, "Thank you. I don't know who you are or where you came from, but thank you."

CHAPTER TWENTY-THREE

September 18, 1996
Wednesday morning

I slept badly. Actually, it's an overstatement to say I slept at all. I flipped and flopped, struggling to get comfortable on the over-used mattress. I took Tylenol, more than directed, and then watched the clock to see when I could take it again. The pain in my shoulder wasn't the problem though. Joanne's murder was.

It had to be Luca or Cray who killed her. I just knew it. But I couldn't figure out how either of them could have done it. Did Luca get away from the Feds? Did Cray have enough time to do it?

The biggest stumbling block was Cray's motive. I was fairly certain he'd overheard me say Joanne was embezzling from him. Was that enough of a reason to kill her? How would he get his money back now that she was dead? And was there enough time to plan the murder if he only decided to kill her that afternoon?

It was still dark when I took a shower. I didn't bother turning on the light, the bathroom felt safer in the dark—or at least cleaner. I threw on a T-shirt and jeans, grabbed my new jacket, filled a bag with a few things, and left. I pretty much had everything with me. My valuables would be safer in the car.

I drove to the 7-Eleven I kept visiting and got a large, bitter coffee, a *Detroit Free Press*, and the mass-produced cinnamon roll I'd almost gotten on Monday—a time that now seemed very far away. Sitting in the rental, I sipped the coffee, read the paper, and ate as much of the cinnamon roll as I could stomach—about half. The front page had a lot of articles about the auto industry. I did not read those. The president was in town campaigning. Violent crime was down by almost ten percent—I imagine Joanne Di Stefano would disagree. Certainly Bob Dole disagreed as he'd been hammering Clinton on crime for weeks. My guess was Republicans took whatever the actual crime figures were and added the deaths they saw on TV the night before and quoted that figure. As long as it seemed like there was a lot of crime they'd win.

I flipped through the whole paper looking for some mention of Joanne's murder. I didn't find anything. It had been two days. Well, one and a half. It should have been in there. It should have been the first story in the local section. But it wasn't. Was one woman's death not considered very important?

Before I left the parking lot, I dumped my trash in a container outside the store and went back in to ask the clerk where Bellagio Drive was. He gave me directions. Well, he kind of gave me directions. He said it was somewhere out near Beck Drive and gave me directions to Beck.

The sun was up, though there was still some pink on the eastern horizon. I'd barely had time to think about it, but the light was different here. And not just that there was more of it in California.

Actually, sometimes there's less of it in LA. When I first ended up there, I noticed summer days seemed shorter than they'd been in Chicago. Eventually, I looked it up. The longest day of light in Los Angeles is a full hour shorter than the longest day of light in Chicago. It must be similar in Michigan. Weird. When you think of California you think of sunshine, but there's actually more of it in the Midwest.

That's what I was thinking about as I took 10 Mile Road out to Beck and turned south. When I found Bellagio Drive, after driving back and forth a few times, I discovered it was behind a gate. Pulling in, I sat staring at the neighborhood. A lot of it was under construction. I couldn't see much, but I could see that. A couple of the homes had been finished but not many. They were enormous. Mansions, really. Brick, two stories, sprawling. The one I could see best had a three-car garage with what were probably maid quarters above. Full grown trees sat in giant wooden boxes waiting to be planted along the street. These people were too rich to wait patiently for trees to grow.

This was where Mr. Cray lived. I suspected he made a decent living squeezing the last dime out of poor people. But nothing like this. No, the people who lived in this neighborhood weren't rich because they had gotten good jobs and worked hard. No, these people started rich and just got richer.

My guess was Cray's money came from his wife. If he'd always been rich he might still be a lawyer, but he'd be working at some ritzy firm where money flowed like ocean currents. Rather than the steady, reliable trickle he'd settled for.

I drove away sure of one thing: Cray didn't care that Joanne was stealing from him. No, if he killed Joanne, something she did Monday afternoon threatened his life on Bellagio Drive.

And then I had to be honest with myself. It might not have been Joanne doing the threatening. It might be me with my questions. If Cray was involved in Dom Reilly's death and he thought I might figure that out, then the life he lived behind the gates would disappear in a flash. If he didn't trust Joanne to keep her mouth shut... he might have killed her.

Was that what the fight between Mr. Cray and Luca was really about? Did Luca think Cray killed Joanne? Was he going to go after Cray? Was I doing this all wrong? Should I just step back and wait for one of them to kill the other? No. I wanted to go home. Waiting around wasn't part of the plan.

I figured I'd learned about as much as I could sitting in front of the gate of a gated community—which was frankly more than I'd expected to. Cray was rich, big rich. Or at least his wife was.

Cruising by Cass's house at around eight-thirty, I saw there were several black-and-white squads out front, and the Crown Vic I'd seen Monday night in the Top Dog parking lot. The garage door was raised. The doors on the Belvedere were open, as was the trunk and the hood. They were doing a thorough job and not finding anything. I imaged they were pissed.

Aunt Suzie's Voyager was in the driveway. She'd done as I'd asked and stayed with Cass. I wondered if she'd slept in the junk room or Cass had allowed her to use Joanne's room.

I drove around the block just to be sure the Feds hadn't come back. It was Luca they were after, or at least that's what I thought. They weren't there so I was probably right.

Then I drove to Top Dog and sat in the parking lot of the storage place next door. It was already after nine so I watched as people arrived for the workday. Mr. Cray arrived around 9:15. I didn't know it was him, though. Not right off. He arrived in a shiny black Porsche 911. His three-car garage made a bit more sense.

What didn't make sense was driving it to work. If the police were putting out that Joanne was killed in a failed carjacking, then why drive a car that was twice as expensive as your everyday car? That only made sense if he knew it wasn't a carjacking.

Claudia arrived around 9:40 in a recent model Honda Prelude. Cherry red. It was so low to the ground she nearly had to crawl to get out of it. I watched as she sauntered into the building, then I drove back to the pay phone at the 7-Eleven, which was quickly becoming my 'office', and called Top Dog. Claudia picked up.

"Hey Claudia, how's it going? This is Nick." Had I told her my name? I couldn't remember.

"Nick who?"

"We've had a couple of chats. I'm the guy who met with Joanne on Monday. I stopped by yesterday."

"Oh. You. What do you want?"

"I'd like to buy you lunch. Twelve o'clock. Anywhere you say."

She didn't think about it, didn't ask what it was about, just jumped at the chance. "There's a restaurant in the Hotel Baronette next to the Twelve Oaks Mall. I've been wanting to go there."

"Then that's where we'll go."

She hung up on me.

I had about an hour and a half. I took a quick trip by Luca's Lifters. The blue Corvette sat out in front. The Feds were down the block. That was as much as I wanted to know, then I drove back to the restaurant.

The Hotel Baronette was a three-story brick building with a concrete awning over the front entrance, and an entrance to Trattoria Bruschetta about thirty feet down. I skipped the valet parking and parked myself in the lot across from the front entrance. The landscaping was pretty nice, with lots of orange and red mums for the fall.

Even from outside I could see that I'd be underdressed for lunch. The collared shirt I'd worn the day before was sitting in a pile on the bathroom floor back at the corporate flophouse. I had almost an hour before lunch so I drove over to the mall, wandered around for a while, then finally went into Hudson's and bought an over-priced, navy blue Izod shirt on Charles Henderson's tab. I found a men's room and put it on.

Then, I drove back to the hotel, parked, and went into the restaurant. It was 11:50. The tablecloths were red and white checks, which made it seem like they were downplaying the upscale nature of the place. The host, a bald guy with a thin mustache and a gold vest, walked me across the plush carpet, put me at a booth against the wall, and laid down two menus.

I glanced at the menu. It looked good but pricey. A waiter, very young and a bit nervous, came by and asked if I'd like a cocktail.

"Do you have lemon soda?"

"Limonata? Yes, we have that."

"Good. I'll have one."

The soda arrived quickly and I sipped it while thinking about the questions I needed to ask Claudia. I had to find out more about Mr. Cray's personal life. If he killed Joanne I needed to know why. I also needed to figure out if he *could* have killed her. Had there been enough time on Monday afternoon for him to be in all the places he needed to be?

My soda was nearly gone when Claudia walked in. The host stopped her and looked as though he might ask her to leave, but she pointed at me and walked by him. As she sat down, I asked if that happened a lot.

"Him? He was just being helpful. I've been helped out of nicer places than this."

She wore a dark purple dress that hugged her curves and a lot of gold jewelry that at least looked real. I hadn't thought much about what she was wearing when I watched her walk in to Top Dog earlier.

"Purple?"

"In honor of Joanne."

"I got the impression you didn't like her much."

"I didn't. If I liked her I'd be wearing black."

The waiter came over and asked Claudia, "Hello, um, would you like a cocktail?"

"I'll have a Cosmo made with your best Japanese vodka. And is there a wine menu?"

"Oh, um, sure... I'll bring one right over." He started to step away, then came back. "Did you want another soda? Sir?"

"Sure."

Before I could decide on my first question, she asked, "Now, who are you again? The last time we talked I neglected to ask who the fuck do you think you are."

I smiled at her belligerence. She wasn't going anywhere until she got her fancy lunch so I relaxed. "I told you. My name is Nick and I'm a friend of the family."

"Joanne's family? You in the Mafia?"

"No." I decided I needed to resort to my cover story. "I'm helping Cass find his father. We met in an AOL chat room for people with missing relatives. Although now I'm trying to help him with what happened to his mother."

"Mmm-hmmm, I've heard about men like you, chatting up teenaged boys on the computer."

"It's not like that. My daughter ran away a few years ago. We found her. She's all right now. People helped me find her so I feel like I should return the favor."

"That's bullshit," she said as the waiter laid the wine menu down in front of her with one hand, and with the other set down a large plate of appetizers: pate, white bean spread, tapenade surrounded by a circle of bruschetta.

"Complimentary hors d'oeuvres. I'll, uh, get your drink. Then, you know, take your order." He scurried off.

Claudia covered one of the tiny slices of toast with a big gob of pate. Before popping it into her mouth, she said, "Go ahead. You want to ask me questions. Ask."

"Mr. Cray seems to have a lot more money than he could earn with a company like Top Dog. Do you know where it comes from?"

She chewed for a moment then swallowed. "His wife. She's from some hoity-toity family around here. Made all their money in glass for windshields, I think. Or maybe carburetors? Doesn't matter I guess."

"With a business like that, they must need lawyers. Why isn't he working for her family?"

After considering that for a moment, she said, "I think they sold it and then her parents died. Or her parents died and then they sold it. I don't remember. Either way, I don't think her family liked Mr. Cray much."

The Cosmo arrived, straight up and bright pink. She looked at the waiter, and said, "Yum." He looked frightened and ran off.

"Do you know why they didn't like Mr. Cray?"

"He's a creep?"

"His wife doesn't think he's a creep, though?"

"You don't know anything about women, do you? Women don't marry a man for who he is, they marry him for who they think he can be. Mr. Cray was a creep with potential."

She took a sip of her drink and closed her eyes in appreciation. I wondered if the waiter had completely forgotten my soda.

"Do you think Mrs. Cray knew about her husband's relationship with Joanne?"

"Depends on what you mean by the word 'know'."

"You said she'd call when Mr. Cray and Joanne went away and try to get their contact information."

"Every time. Didn't really matter, though. Mr. Cray and Joanne always had different rooms. For appearances."

"But you think Mrs. Cray knew about the relationship?"

"And didn't know at the same time."

"What about Mr. Cray? Did he think his wife knew?"

She shook her head. "Men don't know what women think. He thought he had her fooled."

The waiter came back with my second soda. "Would you like to order?"

I'd barely looked at the menu and was about to ask for more time, but Claudia said, "I'd like the rock shrimp, a salad and the veal shank."

The easiest thing to do was say I'd have the same. I really wasn't there for lunch. Once the waiter was gone, I said, "Tell me what happened Monday afternoon, after I left. Did Joanne go in and talk to Mr. Cray?"

"You want to know if you stirred up trouble between them."

"Did I?"

"You did. Right after you left she went into Mr. Cray's office and they had it out, big time. He said he was going to fire her. And she said he'd better not. That he'd be sorry if he tried it."

"As in she'd tell his wife about their affair?"

"Maybe. I couldn't hear that part."

"Did they fight a lot?"

"Enough. They always made up."

"Did they make up on Monday?"

Claudia rolled her eyes. "They sure did. I went to the ladies room. I don't need to hear that kind of thing."

CHAPTER TWENTY-FOUR

September 18, 1996
Wednesday early afternoon

Lunch was delicious. The food came quickly and prevented me from asking more questions. Not that I had many more. When it was time for dessert I declined, but Claudia ordered the tiramisu. She was part way through when I asked, "You said Mr. Cray left right after Joanne on Monday afternoon. What do you mean by 'right after'?"

She pushed her dessert away as though my question had just soured it. "Right after is right after."

"They didn't walk out together?"

"No, I would have said that."

"So, did he leave a minute later or five minutes later?"

"I'm not a clock. I don't know." She did seem to be considering it though. "When Joanne left I was on a call with some deadbeat in Ohio. He was squealing like a stuck pig. Then, when Mr. Cray left, I was giving the guy our address so he could send a check."

"Okay. How does that help me?"

"The calls are scripted. We have two pages of questions and if they haven't offered to send money we threaten to take them to court. When Joanne left, I was already on the second page. Then when Mr. Cray left, I was at the bottom of the page. I'd threatened him with court and he was going to pay."

"Is that about two minutes?"

"Or three, maybe," she said, taking another bite of tiramisu.

"Does Mr. Cray have a gun in his office?"

She looked at me uncomfortably and then swallowed. "Yeah. He does."

"Do you know if it's still there?"

"Now how would I know that? I don't go in his office much. I'm not the maid."

"Could you check?"

Putting down her spoon, she said, "Are you crazy? You think I can't figure out what you're thinking? You think he killed Joanne because she had something on him and she was going to use it? And you want *me* to go and see if he's still got a gun? No way. You're crazy. I'm not getting myself killed for you or anybody else."

She drained the last of the bottle of wine she'd ordered.

"I'm not even going back there. I'm feeling a bad case of food poisoning coming on and it won't go away until I know my boss isn't killing people."

"If you go back and wait until he—"

"Uh-uh, no way. I'm not stupid. I'll pretend to be stupid if I need to, but that's smart. Looking around for some old gun... That's stupid, that's real stupid. Why don't you go in there yourself and be stupid? I'm fine with that."

I left it alone. I couldn't think of even one thing I might have to offer her that would tempt her to go into that office and look for a gun.

Without finishing her dessert, she stood up and said, "Thank you for a lovely lunch. I'm going home now and pretend to be sick."

She walked out of the restaurant with more elegance than a woman who'd just had a Cosmo and a bottle of wine should be able to. After Charles Henderson paid the bill and left a generous tip, I went back to the men's room and relieved myself of the three lemon sodas I had with lunch. There was a pay phone right outside. When I came out, I called Cass's house.

"Are the police gone?"

"Yeah. They left a few minutes ago."

"They didn't find anything, did they?"

"Not really."

"Not really?"

"They tried to take some of my mom's paperwork from the junk room, but Aunt Suzie wouldn't let them."

That had to mean Joanne's financials weren't on the warrant and weren't in plain sight. The fact that they were there looking for evidence in her murder would likely put evidence of crimes she was committing out of bounds.

"You still have my mother's cash?" Cash asked.

"Yeah."

"I want it. And the credit cards."

There was no way I was giving him the cards. He'd end up in prison. And believe it or not, I'd like to end this little adventure with everyone remaining alive and free.

"And the gun. I want the gun back."

"Later. Do you still have a key to Top Dog?"

"Why?"

"Because I'm coming up with a plan."

"Yeah. I have a key. Come and get me."

"I don't want you along for this."

"Then I'm not giving you the key."

Extortion. Blackmail. Kidnapping. The kid had real talent. I hesitated but really I had no choice. "I'll pick you up in a while. I hung up. I had a lot to do.

I drove back to Top Dog. Circling the parking lot, I saw that Mr. Cray's Porsche was there and Claudia's Prelude was not. Then I drove two office buildings down. The building was nearly identical to the one that housed Top Dog. I parked in the back in roughly the spot where Mr. Cray's BMW would have been. I turned the car off then stared at the clock. It was digital. As soon as it turned 1:34 I jumped out of the car and quickly walked into the building I bolted up the stairs to the second floor. Part way down the hallway I decided which office matched Top Dog. It had taken me roughly thirty-seconds to get there.

Then I hurried down the hallway to the men's room at the front of the building. I stepped inside and stood in a booth. I pretended to open a briefcase, take out a hoodie, put it on, pick up a gun and set the briefcase on the back of the toilet. I left the bathroom, hurried down the stairs to the first floor, and walked out of it building.

I went directly to the spot that corresponded with where Joanne's car had been. I pretended to shoot her and then pick up her purse. I hurried back to the building and climbed the stairs to the first floor. Then I 'took off' the hoodie, imagined standing on the toilet and putting the stolen purse in the ceiling, and went back into the booth where I 'picked up' the briefcase and put the gun and the hoody into it. I added extra time because the hoodie barely fit.

Then I went back out to the hallway and walked to the back of the building, down the stairs and out to the Thunderbird. I got into the car and looked at the clock. It said 1:37. Three minutes. Roughly.

I tried to remember what I'd seen on the video. Joanne was killed at 4:56 and then Mr. Cray got into this BMW at around 5:02. Six minutes. I'd done it in three. He could have dawdled. He could have taken his time. Most importantly, he could have done it. He could have killed her. There was enough time.

Looking at it another way, he'd walked out of the office about three minutes after Joanne. She'd come out of the building at 4:51. Mr. Cray should have come out the back of the building at 4:54. There were eight unaccounted for minutes.

I got out of the car, walked around and opened the trunk, and took a thousand dollars out of the shoebox. Then I walked around the first building until I found Rocky mopping the upstairs hallway.

"I'm seeing a lot of you," was the first thing he said.

"This should be it. I don't think you'll see me after today. I've got a thousand dollars for you."

"Out of the goodness of your heart?"

"I need you to do something."

"For a thousand dollars? Is it illegal?"

"Probably not."

He laughed and shook his head. "Probably not. Oh, that's a good one."

"Look, it's very likely no one will ever know. There's only a small chance it might become... a thing."

With a frown he asked, "What do you need me to do?"

"I need you to turn off all the cameras covering the Top Dog building from five-forty-five to six-fifteen. That's all."

"That's all?"

"If things go well, no one will ever ask to see the missing video. Nobody's going to get hurt. I'm trying to catch a killer, that's all."

"That's all," he said again.

I felt myself blushing. I didn't do that much anymore so it was a bit embarrassing. The way I was talking about all this was much more casual than I felt. I was having trouble resisting the temptation to beg.

"What if it doesn't go well?" he asked.

"That's up to you. You can make up a plausible story or you can tell the truth. Some guy gave you money to turn the cameras off."

He thought about it. I thought about it too. I was asking him to take a chance I wasn't willing to take myself. If everything went to plan it wouldn't matter if the cameras were on or off. I stood there anxiously hoping he wouldn't figure that out, promising myself I'd make it up to him if things went wrong.

"Five-forty-five to six-fifteen?"

"Yes."

"Will I see you later?"

"Hopefully not."

When I got to Cass's house he came out and got into the Thunderbird. His aunt's van was in the driveway.

"What's your aunt doing?" I asked.

"Cleaning up. The cops left a mess."

"That's nice of her. Did you help?"

"I didn't ask her to do it."

"That doesn't mean you shouldn't help."

He ignored me, and asked, "Where's the shoebox with the money?"

"In the trunk. I've had to use a couple thousand for expenses."

"What expenses?"

"Bribing people isn't cheap."

"Where's the gun?"

"In my pocket. Where it's going to stay."

"And the credit cards?"

"I'm not giving those back to you."

"What? They're mine!"

"Technically, they're not."

"What am I going to live on?"

"The papers the cops wanted to take, did you look at them?"

"No."

"Why not?"

"Felt wrong. My mom was kind of private."

I sighed. "She had a lot of bank accounts. The statements were in the junk room. She might even have more that I didn't find. I didn't do what I'd call an extensive search. Between the bank accounts and whatever you make selling the house you should have plenty of money. Enough to go to college even."

"Fuck college."

"Or you can stay in your bedroom playing Donkey Kong until you're ready for a mid-life crisis."

"I don't play Donkey Kong. It's stupid."

I shrugged. Honestly, I didn't even know what Donkey Kong was except I'd heard a while back that kids were playing too much of it.

"So what's the plan?" Cass asked.

"We're going to do to Cray what he was going to do to you. We're going to put the gun and the hoodie in his office and then let the police know they're there."

He thought about that for a moment, and said, "Cool."

"But first we're going back inside to help your aunt clean up."

"What? No, she's okay."

"We've got a couple of hours."

He rolled his eyes and got out of the Thunderbird. Following him into the house, I could easily figure out how the search had gone. They'd started in the garage with Cass's car where they'd been told the gun and hoodie would be. When those weren't there, they'd have worked their way through the garage and into the house. By the time they got to the front of the house, the dining room and living room, they were pretty angry. There was a coat closet next to the front door. Its contents were now strewn on the floor. In the living room, both sofas were flipped over, the liquor cabinet stood open, and the carpet was rolled back. In the dining room, the China closet doors stood open and the shelves empty, confirming my suspicion that they hadn't held any serving items. Cass and I flipped the sofas upright. Aunt Suzie could not have done that on her own. I glanced at the den, which looked like Aunt Suzie had already straightened up in there.

We went into the kitchen and found her there. She was standing in front of the counter wearing a pink bowling shirt that said PINK LADIES on the back and Suzie Q over her right breast. There was food all over the counter. The refrigerator stood open and was completely empty. When she saw us she said, "Why would they have to search the refrigerator?"

"It's not a bad place to hide a gun."

"And why were they looking for a gun? They can't seriously think Cassidy would..."

"Someone called in a tip. They had to check it out."

"They took a couple of Cassidy's hoodies."

"What colors?"

"Red and blue," Cass answered for her.

"No Spartan green?"

"My mom didn't like sports," he said. And then for a brief moment I saw a light in his eye that suggested he was realizing he could now like sports if he wanted to.

"They're going to test the hoodies for gunshot residue. They won't find anything."

"Cassidy, why don't you go upstairs and put your room back together," Aunt Suzie suggested. Honestly, I didn't remember his room looking 'together' before the search.

He looked from me to his aunt and back again. Clearly, he was deciding whether we'd be talking about anything he cared about. He went with not caring, and said, "Fine. Whatever."

She nodded her head toward the backyard and walked over to the slider. She went out to the patio and I followed her.

"What's up?" I asked.

"This is none of your business. What I'm going to tell you, it's not your business. But you should know. I guess."

Confusing, if it wasn't my business then I really shouldn't know. She looked upset though.

"What is it?"

"I just... I'm hoping you can help with Cass."

"Sure."

I was beginning to think someone was dying of cancer.

"Hector, the young man who was with Heather. You met him? Yesterday."

"Yeah."

"He says he's Cassidy's father."

"Okay. Do you believe him?"

"I think so. I never thought Cassidy looked much like my family. But I thought that was the Sicilian in him. Dominant, you know?"

"Do you think your brother knew?"

"It wouldn't have mattered if he did. He loved Cassidy so much."

"What about you?"

"Me? Well... oh, you're asking... He's my nephew. Always will be."

"Are you going to tell him?"

"It doesn't seem fair not to. I mean, losing his mom, growing up without a dad. It doesn't seem right not to tell him he still has a father."

"How do you think he'll take it?"

"I don't know. I'm a little worried."

And that was the point of telling me something that was none of my business. She wanted me to help with this if I could. I told her, "I'm hoping I'll be able to go back to... home. Tomorrow, possibly."

"I want to be the one to tell him. I want him to know that Dominick loved him, no matter. I'll tell him soon."

She looked bleak for a moment and then went back into the house. I went back in and straightened things up in the living and dining rooms. When I was done with that I went up to Cass's room to tell him it was time to go. The room looked like Kansas after a tornado.

"What did Aunt Suzie want to talk to you about?"

"She wants me to encourage you to go to college."

He stewed for a moment. "Well go ahead, say whatever you got to say."

"It's really not my business. If you want to be a plumber or a janitor, go ahead."

"I'm not going to do either of those things."

"I doubt Mr. Cray will keep you on. Not if we get him sent to prison. Speaking of which, we need to go."

According to the clock on the dashboard of the Thunderbird it was 5:40 when we reached Top Dog. I drove up and down in front of the building until it was 5:46. Then we drove into the parking lot and circled the building. When I was sure Mr. Cray had gone home for the day, we parked. I opened the trunk and grabbed the bag with the hoodie and the gun. Then we entered the building.

We were quickly up the stairs to the second floor. Cass took out his keys and we were in the office. Mr. Cray's office was a tiny bit larger than Joanne's, and a bit nicer, mostly in that his fake wood was nicer fake wood than hers. There were a half a dozen photos of his family sitting on the credenza. His wife was pretty but washed-out looking— she didn't have anything like the fire Joanne had. She was still alive though. Maybe fire wasn't that desirable. There were four kids in the photos. The oldest boy wore a Spartans T-shirt. He was probably the original owner of the hoodie. He might have left it at the office while visiting. Or maybe he'd left it in his father's car. I wasn't sure about that.

Taking my new jacket off and laying it on the chair, I climbed up onto the desk, pushed one of the panels out of the way and reached down for the bag. I had clamped down on my jaw since raising my hands above my head was often painful. I promised myself another Tylenol as soon as I got down.

Before I took the bag, I stopped. "Your fingerprints are on the bag. Wrap the gun in the hoody and then hand them up to me."

"What about fingerprints on the hoody?"

"It's pretty impossible to lift prints off fabric. Make sure we take the bag with us."

He handed me the hoodie-wrapped gun and I slipped it into the space above me. I was reaching for the ceiling tile to pull back into place when the office door opened. I looked down and there was Mr. Cray.

"What exactly is it you're doing? Never mind, I know what you're doing."

Cass seemed to spring awake. He picked up my jacket and reached into the pocket pulling out the Ruger. He clumsily aimed it at Mr. Cray, but the man was already rushing Cass. He slammed the boy up against the credenza behind the desk. Then he snatched the gun out of his hand. I can't say I was surprised. Mr. Cray stepped back, aiming the gun at us. We all focused on our breathing for a moment.

"Did you forget something?" I asked, curious to know if this was simply bad luck.

"Blue Thunderbird. I saw it as I was leaving. I remembered seeing it yesterday at Joanne's. I doubled back to see if it was here. And there it was in my parking space. And here you are in my office."

"You killed my mom," Cass said, petulant, sulky and powerless.

"Your mom was a deceitful bitch. You need to come to terms with that."

Before Cass could respond to that, I asked, "If she was so awful why were you with her for so long?"

"We understood each other. Good people are so boring. My wife is a lovely person. Kind, generous, thoughtful, bland, dull, boring. I will miss Joanne. She was a deceitful bitch, and I loved her."

"You killed my father, didn't you?"

"Oh for god's sake, why does that matter so much? You realize none of this would have happened if you hadn't started nosing around. You barely knew the man."

That was a lot for Cass to take in, but he pulled himself together and said, "I wanted to know him. And I couldn't... because of you."

"Yes, I had your father killed. That's what Joanne wanted so I paid her cousin to do it. Stupid of me, really. I think Luca would have done it for free if she'd asked. As it was, I think she kept most of the ten thousand dollars I paid for him to do it. You'd have thought getting rid of a husband she didn't want would have been enough. But that was Joanne for you. Why place one bet when you can place two?"

For a moment, I thought about reaching up and grabbing the other gun, but I couldn't imagine a way in which he wouldn't shoot me before I even got my hands on it. And then he was saying, "Well, I've told you my secrets. Now it's time for you to die."

He aimed the gun at Cass, I braced myself to watch the kid die. And then wait for my turn. Mr. Cray pulled the trigger and the gun clicked. And nothing happened. He pointed the gun down and looked at the safety. Then he began pulling at the slide.

Meanwhile, I was reaching for the gun above my head, so I wasn't looking when the Ruger went off. I turned to see that Mr. Cray had shot himself, somewhere in the thigh region. Cass jumped forward and grabbed the gun out of his hand. Good boy. I got the gun down from the ceiling but didn't take it out of the hoodie.

"I'm bleeding. Call an ambulance," Mr. Cray said.

To Cass, I said, "Don't try to fire that again. It'll probably misfire."

Mr. Cray had both hands around his thigh, squeezing hard as blood seeped through his fingers. There was already blood on the floor around his feet.

"Call an ambulance," he said again.

"It won't get here in time," I said.

I took the gun from Cass and rubbed my fingers all over the spots where his had been. Hopefully, I made such a smudgy enough mess that neither of us would be identified. I tossed it into the pool of blood surrounding Mr. Cray. He stared at it a moment, then his knees folded and he slumped onto the floor.

I'd been right. There was no way he'd live until an ambulance arrived. I didn't think he'd even live long enough to get to the telephone. To Cass I said, "I think it's time for us to leave. Don't step in the blood."

The two of us carefully picked our way out of the office. As we did, Mr. Cray said his last words. "Wait... please... fuck."

In the reception area I checked Cass over. There was a fine spray of blood on his clothes, but he wasn't tracking any blood on the floor. And neither was I.

We left and went down the stairs to the first floor. Cass started to get into the rental but I stopped him. "Hold on." I walked back to the trunk. I had a few T-shirts from a pack and some underwear.

"Ditch those clothes and put these on. Make sure you don't leave anything in the pockets."

"You want me to go around in my underwear?"

"You're covered in little specs of blood. And we're going right to your place as soon as I do one more thing."

I could see he wanted to argue, but then he collapsed under the weight of the situation. "Yeah. Whatever."

I took the shoebox out of the trunk and closed it. Then I walked over to the storage facility next door and found the control room again. Rocky was sitting inside. Several of the screens in front of him were blank. He'd done as I asked.

Seeing me he said, "Oh, shit."

"Yeah. Things went sideways."

"What does that mean?"

I held out the shoebox. "There's ten or twelve thousand dollars in here. I haven't counted it. There's a dead guy in the Top Dog office. He accidentally shot himself. In about a half an hour, discover his body. Say you heard a shot. Eventually the police will want to look at the missing video. Tell them a guy in a blue Corvette with a white stripe paid you to turn it off. In a few days, leave town. San Diego. Anywhere you want to go."

"There's no other way to play this?"

"You could tell the truth, I suppose. You don't know my real name. But the guy with the Corvette deserves to be in jail. You could help send him there."

"But it's scary enough that I have to leave town."

"That's true."

"I won't come back to testify."

"I don't think you'll need to. By that time they'll have enough real evidence to put the guy away for good."

He reached out and took the shoebox from me. We wished each other luck and then I left.

Cass was sitting in the car in his underwear—well, my underwear. Despite being dry, he managed to look like an unhappy wet dog.

"Did we just kill a man?" he asked.

I wondered what answer he wanted to hear. Would he be happier if I said, 'Yes, we killed a man?' I decided on the truth. "We didn't know the gun would malfunction. We didn't know he'd get it away from you. You could have easily been the one bleeding to death on that floor."

Before I'd even got us out of the parking lot, he said, "We have to kill Luca."

"No. We don't need to do that. The security guard is going to tell the police that Luca was the one who paid him to have the cameras turned off. The gun that Mr. Cray shot himself with was owned by Luca's former girl-friend. You told me that. And it may have been used to kill a judge. There's a lot of holes, but I trust the police to fill them in. Luca's going to prison. Probably for the rest of his life."

"He deserves to die."

"He deserves to suffer. Death ends suffering."

CHAPTER TWENTY-FIVE

September 19, 1996
Thursday

In the morning, I drove over to Aunt Suzie's house to say good-bye before I went to the airport. The purple Civic was in the driveway. I was pretty sure it belonged to Heather.

I'd actually slept well. Particularly well, despite watching a man die. I tried to feel bad about it. But no matter how I looked at it, he'd basically killed himself. Yeah, I was the one who apparently hadn't cleaned the gun well enough. But I never suggested that Mr. Cray take it away from Cass and try to shoot him. He'd done that willingly. I also wasn't the one who'd buried the gun. I was just the one who missed some of the dirt. An honest mistake.

"We just heard about Mr. Cray," Aunt Suzie said when she opened the door. "The police came by. Wanted to know where Cass was last night."

"What did he say?"

"*I* said he was with me."

I nodded. "So, Mr. Cray is dead?"

"Don't act like you didn't know." Then she patted me on the arm. I thought she might say something like 'good job' or 'well done.' I resisted the temptation to explain it had all been an accident.

"Did they say anything about Luca?"

"They're looking for him. He must have given the Feds the slip."

Which was perfect. Cass came out and Aunt Suzie said, "Well, I'll give you two a moment."

He stepped out and closed the door. Just as well, I didn't really want to be invited in. "So, are we done?" I asked. "I can go home and you'll leave Dom Reilly alone?"

"I wasn't really gonna do anything to you."

I did not believe that for a moment, but didn't correct him.

"They're saying that Hector guy is my real dad."

"Oh, wow," I said, because it was appropriate to the situation—and also because I was surprised Aunt Suzie had moved things long that quickly. "I guess I see the resemblance."

Cass just scowled.

"That's not a bad thing. The guy's pretty good-looking. Maybe his genes will kick in soon."

He gave me the side-eye before saying, "He's Mexican."

"Yeah, and apparently so are you."

"My mom's family's gonna hate that."

I decided not to touch that one.

"Does Hector want to be your dad?"

"That's what he says."

"How's your Aunt Suzie taking this?"

"That I'm Mexican?"

"That she's not really your aunt." Of course, I knew the answer already, I just wanted to make the point to Cass.

"Oh she says she'll be my aunt no matter what."

"Sounds like you've got some good people looking out for you."

He squinted at me in the sunlight before saying, "You were like my dad for a week, weren't you?"

"You had to blackmail me into it."

"Well not real—okay, maybe a little."

When I said good-bye, the little creep actually hugged me. That got me a little choked up, which was stupid. If I thought logically, I never wanted to see this kid again as long as I lived. And I also hoped that he'd be okay and that people would start taking better care of him.

On the way to the airport, I found a big garbage bin in an alley and tossed away all the things I'd acquired—including Joanne's collection of fraudulent credit cards. I couldn't guarantee that some homeless person wouldn't find them while digging through for cans... Well, good for them.

I got to the airport and dropped the Thunderbird off with Hertz. It took nearly an hour to find a flight after checking in at three different airlines. The best I could do was standby with United—and that only went to Dallas. After I didn't get on the first flight, I went to a newsstand for something to read. It was just a few days ago I'd bought *K Is for Killer*. Somewhere along the line I'd lost it. I wasn't sure where. I'd barely read the first chapter.

Looking at the available books, I struggled. After the week I'd had I wasn't in the mood for John Grisham or Michael Crichton. I would have liked something light and funny, but there didn't seem to be much like that. I ended up with *Mindhunter*, a true story about serial killers. Hardly light and funny, but at least different from the things I faced over the last week.

Once on the plane, I was deep into my bag of nuts when I realized I'd be traveling for about double the time it took to fly direct. That was not a great thought. I tried to focus on the book I'd bought, but my mind kept slipping back to the week I'd just spent in Michigan. I was sure I'd made some missteps, probably some big ones. I was hoping, praying even, that once the police had the bright and shiny Luca Amato in their sights they wouldn't bother too much with the guy who'd been floating around trying not to give people his name.

During the layover, I considered calling Ronnie. But I worried that if he was mad, and he had every right to be, he might say some pretty horrible things to me, things that would be hard to walk back. I figured it would harder to say unforgivable things to my face. And easier to forgive.

When I finally arrived in Los Angeles it was past eight and the sun had been down for about an hour and a half. As I was waiting for the shuttle to Lot B, I noticed a trash bin. I walked over and dumped Charles Henderson's credit card and temporary license. I sincerely hoped he'd never see a bill and never have to pay for the damage I'd done to his balance.

It was less than a half an hour from the airport to Long Beach. Rush hour had ended an hour before. When I got to our neighborhood, I drove around for another ten minutes looking for a parking space. Normally, that would have driven me up the wall. But that night I almost didn't want to find a spot. But I did. Four blocks away.

My front door was unlocked. A blessing since I hadn't been looking forward to knocking on my own door. When I walked in, Junior and John were there sitting with Ronnie at the dining table. They were playing cards. When he saw me, Junior said, "I'm teaching them three-handed pinocle."

"Why?" I asked.

"Because card games are just what the doctor ordered when someone disappears for a week."

I wanted to kill him, but I was too busy dying myself. Every second that Ronnie didn't get up and come over to me was killing me. He was staring at me but he wasn't budging.

Trying to change the direction of the conversation, I asked, "So what did I miss?"

"The upstairs bathroom sprang a leak," Junior said. "I was the one who discovered it. The wall in the stairwell began seeping blood."

"Rust from the pipes," John said.

"Well, it looked just like blood."

"Sounds expensive," I said.

"It's fine," Ronnie said.

Still, I felt guilty. I'd put several thousand dollars on our credit card. Ronnie had one he kept just for the houses, but it still was going to be a challenge to get them all paid down again.

"The plumber though..." Junior said. "Perfection."

"Junior kept making passes at him," John said.

"I did *not*."

"You mentioned you're single at least three times."

"That's considered a pass? My god, in the seventies you'd have to get on your knees and unzip someone's pants before it qualified as a pass."

Then Ronnie said, "All right boys. Evening's over."

"Well, I never—" Junior started to say.

John said, "Don't."

"... I never got to say how much we miss having you two around the house."

"Well, now you've said it. We should go," John said.

The two of them got up and quietly walked out of the apartment.

Ronnie picked up some glasses they'd been using and took them into the kitchen. When he returned, he said, "I told everyone you had a family emergency in Michigan. I don't think anyone believed me."

"It's a bit vague."

"When you think up a better lie, make sure to tell me."

Yikes, that was bad.

"I'm sorry."

"Lydia's desperate for you to call. They've got a bunch of new cases. Something about a jailhouse snitch in Orange County."

"She told you that?"

"It was in the newspaper."

"Really? That seems—"

"Edwin jumped the gun. She's pissed."

"I'll call tomorrow. Ronnie—"

"You disappeared two days ago. Completely disappeared."

"Um. What do you mean? I left last Friday."

"You were in Reno for a few hours with that kid and then the two of you got on a flight to Detroit. I don't know where you stayed Saturday night, but I do know you ate at a Taco Bell—you hate Taco Bell."

"I do."

Ronnie loved Taco Bell. It was a bone of contention.

"Sunday morning you went to a place called The Clock Diner. You weren't alone. You took a trip to K-Mart and bought a lot of stuff. Sunday night you stayed at a Motel 6. The next morning you were back at The Clock Diner. Then you disappeared. Yesterday this arrived."

From a drawer in our China closet he took out the FedEx package I'd sent. Opened.

I said, "It should have gotten here on Tuesday. I sent it overnight."

"You sent your ID and credit card home."

"I needed to be someone else for a few days."

He stared at me for a moment. He'd been a good little detective. I suspected he was much better at this than I'd ever thought. In his spot, I'd have done the same.

"How did you pay for your ticket home?"

"Just a touch of fraud."

"Can it be traced back to you?"

"I don't think so." Then I decided to be more definitive, "No. I'm sure it can't be."

We were quiet for a long, uncomfortable moment. I couldn't stop myself from saying, "I'm sorry, Ronnie. I had to go... I promise I'll make it up to you.

"There are things I don't know about you. A lot of things. But I *do* know you. You wouldn't have left like that to help some kid you didn't know. Not without talking to me. You did what you did for us. For me."

"That's right," I said, because it was right

Taking a step forward, he reached up and touched my face.

"Then welcome home."

EPILOGUE

Fall 1982

The apartment wasn't very nice. The walls were paneled in dark, make-believe walnut. The young woman's four-year-old was crying in the living room. She got out of bed, taking the sheets with her, opened the bedroom door, and yelled at him. Then she went back to the bed.

"You need to go soon," she said to the young man beside her. She kissed him again, and whispered, "You're going to do it for me, aren't you?"

"Why don't you just divorce him, Jojo?"

"Then he'll always be around wanting to see the kid."

"But you could get remarried if you got divorced."

"I don't want to get remarried."

"What if I want to marry you?"

"Don't be gross. You're my cousin."

"What are you talking about? You'll have sex with me but you won't marry me?"

"Sex is nobody's business. Marriage is everybody's business." She sat up and put on her bra. "Look, if you don't want to do it, don't do it."

"I didn't say that."

"It's a good deal. Mr. Cray is good for the money."

"Are you fucking him?"

"No. He's paying you two thousand dollars to get rid of my husband out of the goodness of his heart. Of course, I'm fucking him. And don't get all jealous about it. This is good for you."

"Doesn't he want to marry you?"

"God no. His wife comes from money and she gets it all when her parents die. He's gotta stay married to her. And maybe I don't want to marry him. Maybe I don't want to marry anyone."

"You won't be able to. Not if he disappears."

The young woman smiled at him. "That's what I want though. I want him to disappear, like he was never here at all. I want you to be my magician."

"Don't worry, Jojo. I'll do magic for you."

ALSO BY MARSHALL THORNTON

IN THE BOYSTOWN MYSTERIES SERIES

Boystown: Three Nick Nowak Mysteries

Boystown 2: Three More Nick Nowak Mysteries

Boystown 3: Two Nick Nowak Novellas

Boystown 4: A Time for Secrets

Boystown 5: Murder Book

Boystown 6: From the Ashes

Boystown 7: Bloodlines

Boystown 8: The Lies That Bind

Boystown 9: Lucky Days

Boystown 10: Gifts Given

Boystown 11: Heart's Desire

Boystown 12: Broken Cord

Boystown 13: Fade Out

The Boystown Prequels

IN THE PINX VIDEO MYSTERIES SERIES

Night Drop

Hidden Treasures

Late Fees

Rewind

Cash Out

Help Wanted

Kapowie!

IN THE DOM REILLY SERIES

Year of the Rat

A Mean Season

The Happy Month

A Week Away

IN THE WYANDOT COUNTY SERIES

The Less Than Spectacular Times of Henry Milch

A Fabulously Unfabulous Summer for Henry Milch

The Fall and Rise of Henry Milch

OTHER BOOKS

The Perils of Praline

Desert Run

Full Release

The Ghost Slept Over

My Favorite Uncle

Femme

Praline Goes to Washington

Aunt Belle's Time Travel & Collectibles

Masc

Never Rest

Code Name: Liberty

Fathers of the Bride

Sentenced to Christmas

ABOUT THE AUTHOR

Marshall Thornton writes several popular mystery series, most notably the *Boystown Mysteries* and the *Pinx Video Mysteries*. He has won the Lambda Award for Gay Mystery three times. His books *Femme* and *Code Name Liberty* were Lambda finalists for Best Gay Romance. Other books include *My Favorite Uncle*, *The Ghost Slept Over* and *Fathers of the Bride*. He holds an MFA in Screenwriting from UCLA.